LASSO KUMBH

THE SPIRIT, THE RITUAL, AND THE CURSE

AZITEJ ANAND

I dedicate this book to the cherished memory of my beloved late parents, whose blessings have been the guiding light of my life. To all my dear ones who stood by me with unwavering support and encouragement throughout this journey—this achievement would not have been possible without you.

With heartfelt gratitude, I humbly offer this work as a tribute to your love and belief in me.

Contents

Foreword

Books possess a unique power to transcend time, weaving narratives that echo through generations. 'Lasso Kumbh' is one such masterpiece—a profound blend of history, spirituality, and intrigue that takes readers on a journey through the untold corridors of the past.

Azitej Anand's storytelling is nothing short of extraordinary, inviting readers into a world where the mystical and the historical collide. Through its vivid descriptions and hauntingly beautiful prose, this work delves into the unexplored corners of our cultural memory, blending folklore, rituals, and human resilience into a compelling narrative.

As you turn these pages, prepare to be immersed in a tale that challenges the boundaries of history and myth. This is not just a story; it is an experience—a dance of time where each step reveals a secret, and every twist leaves you yearning for more.

To embark on this journey is to embrace the unknown, to question the familiar, and to emerge with a perspective forever transformed. I invite you to open your heart and mind to the world of 'Lasso Kumbh'—a story that will resonate with your soul long after the final chapter.

Welcome to the extraordinary.

Preface

History has always been a tapestry woven with threads of mystery, legend, and untold truths. Beneath the surface of recorded events lie stories shrouded in shadows, waiting to be unearthed. These tales are not just forgotten chapters of the past—they are keys to understanding our present and glimpses into the uncharted realms of human experience.

'**Lasso Kumbh**', is born from this belief, a journey into a world where the spiritual, historical, and mystical converge. It seeks to illuminate the unseen, to bring forth the voices silenced by time, and to explore the delicate dance between the supernatural and the human spirit.

At its heart, this book is a reflection on the complexities of history: the way it is written, remembered, and sometimes deliberately concealed. It challenges the boundaries between reality and myth, science and superstition, and invites readers to question the narratives they have always known.

As you step into the pages of '**Lasso Kumbh**', prepare to embark on a journey unlike any other. It is a voyage through forgotten villages, ancient rituals, and the timeless interplay of light and darkness. This is not merely a story but an invitation to reimagine history and confront the mysteries that dwell within its folds.

I hope this book inspires curiosity, ignites introspection, and leaves you with a renewed sense of wonder for the enigmas of time and existence. Welcome to the world of '**Lasso Kumbh**'. The journey begins here.

Acknowledgements

With immense gratitude and a heart brimming with appreciation, I extend my thanks to the countless sources of inspiration that shaped **Lasso Kumbh**.

To the stories embedded in history, folklore, and the whispers of timeless traditions—your essence became the lifeblood of this narrative. The dance of time, the spirit of resilience, and the shadows of forgotten truths brought this tale to life, weaving a fabric of mystery, depth, and revelation.

I am profoundly thankful to my family and friends, whose unwavering belief in my vision has been my anchor and my guiding light. Your encouragement and support allowed me to dream beyond the horizon and bring this manuscript to fruition.

To the readers and storytellers who walk the delicate bridge between reality and imagination—this book is for you. Your curiosity fuels the timeless exploration of stories yet untold, and it is your passion that keeps the written word alive and thriving.

Finally, to the unseen forces of inspiration—the spirit of creativity, the mystery of history, and the enduring power of storytelling—thank you for igniting the spark that made **Lasso Kumbh** possible.

May this book resonate with your spirit and stir the unseen within us all.

With deepest appreciation,
Azitej Anand

Prologue

The air was thick with a silence that hummed, a silence that spoke louder than words. It was the kind of stillness that clung to the shadows, where the whisper of the unknown lingers, daring you to listen. Time itself seemed to falter, caught in the gravity of a story waiting to be unveiled—a story carved into the very bones of history, hidden beneath layers of ritual, power, and a curse that defied the logic of the living.

Far away, beyond the veil of modern understanding, lay the village of Munda. In its heart burned a fire of tradition, flickering on the edges of survival. But even the brightest of flames cast the darkest shadows. Beneath the surface of the village's vibrant life simmered whispers of dread—stories of the **Lasso Kumbh**, a ritual as old as time and twice as relentless.

The curse was said to be born of desperate faith, a forgotten pact forged in the dim corridors of history. And now, like a phantom from the past, it was stirring once more, calling forth a chain of events that would threaten to unravel everything.

In this land of ancient wisdom and forbidden rituals, one man stood at the crossroads of destiny. Gaurakhi, a seeker bound by fate and faith, walked the perilous line between the mortal and the divine. He carried with him questions that could not be ignored and answers that the world might not be ready to hear.

This is not merely a tale of ghosts or gods, rituals or curses. It is the untold story of history's shadow, where truth and myth collide, where the present dances with the echoes of a forgotten past. And as the winds shift and the first strains of a forgotten melody fill the air, one question lingers:

When time itself takes a breath, what truths will emerge from the depths of the **Lasso Kumbh?**

CHAPTER ONE

The Shadow

"Everything that happens may be destined for a greater good, but often, even in the journey toward goodness, shadows of unforeseen tragedies linger, reminding us that even noble paths are paved with moments of darkness."
History tells us that it twists and turns in ways that no one has ever seen or understood.

The story begins in a small village, where one man is speaking to another. Their conversation marks the start of an unfolding tale—a journey into the unknown, woven with mystery and destiny. The air is thick with anticipation as the words exchanged between them set the stage for what lies ahead.

" Do you know? It's happening again, just like before. The **Lasso Kumbh —but this time, we don't know which innocent life is at stake. The Lasso Kumbh** seems to have transformed, as if it has become a deadly well, a trap from which escape seems impossible. Yet, there is no choice—we must survive. The pace of crafting clay lamps in the village seemed to grow faster with each passing day. The new moon was approaching, and an unspoken dread hung in the air—no one knew which household the storm of misfortune would descend upon this time. It felt as though every new moon forced the villagers to celebrate it as if it were Diwali. Truth be told, it had become nearly impossible to tell when the true Diwali had come and gone amidst these endless *"Small Diwalis."*

Only the biting cold of winter served as a reminder of the real festival of lights, marked by the distinct absence of these fragile, featherless clay lamps. "Let's go," one of them muttered, as they looked at the overcast sky. "We should gather the clay before it rains too hard tonight. Otherwise, today's wings of cracked earth will be too scattered to use."

"You're right," said the other.

Without another word, the two men bent down, gathering handfuls of soil near the village of mandu. They worked with quiet efficiency, their hands caked in the wet earth as they prepared to bring it back home—a ritual that had become as natural as breathing.

Thus began their work under the sullen sky, unaware of the larger storm brewing both within their village and beyond.

Look, the rope is standing upright, emerging from the pot, as if defying all natural laws. The **Lasso Kumbh** begins once again, the cycle repeating, the danger looming..."

The story begins in 1770's...

At this time, while British power was solidifying its rule over India, death had become so cheap that even calculating it seemed absurd. The scarcity caused by the changing seasons and the lack of accurate weather knowledge had driven humanity to the brink of death. On one side, the decline of the Mughal Empire, which had begun after 1707, was apparent, while on the other, the British were taking full advantage of the opportunity to expand. The Nawab of Bengal, **Siraj ud-Daulah**, was defeated, and the right to collect revenue from the region was granted to the Mughal Emperor **Shah Alam** following the **Battle of Buxar.** India was witnessing events like the **Battle of Plassey** and **the Buxar Rebellion**, which prompted the East India Company to implement the Regulating Act to manage the country effectively.

At this crossroads, the region of what is now West Bengal, including parts of Orissa, Bihar, and Jharkhand, emerged as an economic hub brimming with potential.The village of **Mandu,** much like any other village in the region, lay in the heart of the Santhal Parganas. After the events of the Santhal rebellion, the village's name was changed from **Mandu** to **Munda,** in honor of the great Birsa Munda. Yet, some held the belief that both Birsa Munda and Barphukan, like many others, were born from this very soil. **Mandu** or

Munda—these names were but pages of history, shaping the identity of a village that had been moulded by two distinct legacies. Those who held the village's history close, still referred to it by its old name, **Mandu.

Under the shadow of the British empire, **Mandu**, much like other princely regions, had been reduced to nothing more than a puppet kingdom, its ruler nothing more than a figurehead, a mere marionette under the control of foreign dominion. The British had nurtured the dream of bringing every village, including this one, under their iron grasp. **Mandu** too had found itself caught in the grip of British power, as the English had brought the might of their empire to bear on this land.

The once-proud kingdom, led by its Raja, had been slowly stripped of its sovereignty, and by the end of the 18th century, the **Permanent Settlement** had rendered the Raja almost impotent, as if the very essence of power had been drained from him. The Raja, though still on the throne, had become little more than a shadow of his former self, powerless before the overwhelming might of the British.

The combined weight of the Raja's impotence and the unchecked authority of the British left the village in a state of paralysis, with its spirit crushed under the heel of colonial rule. The village of **Mandu**, had been reduced to mere ashes of its former self, a place where the echoes of its past greatness were all but drowned by the relentless tide of foreign control.

The story starts in a small village named Mandu. This village, situated in a region struggling with an unusual crisis, was grappling with a famine. The English government, indifferent to the villagers' plight, dismissed their suffering as a result of the changing weather. Despite the obvious signs of death and despair, the villagers sensed a more sinister force at play, one that went beyond the mere shortage of food. They were convinced that a dark power was behind their suffering, a malevolent force that the British authorities refused to acknowledge.

The village was haunted by the unexplained deaths of women and children, which the villagers attributed to this dark force. Yet, under British rule, such beliefs were disregarded, and the authorities were too preoccupied with their own issues to address the villagers' concerns. The government's disdainful response following the 'Black Hole' incident had left them in a state of desperation, often ignoring their pleas for help. Faced with this, what were the villagers to do?

Gaurakhi, who traced his lineage to the revered Gaurakhnath dynasty, was a seeker on a sacred journey. Devoted to the worship of Lord Shiva, he embarked on a solitary path toward the mighty Himalayas. His purpose was clear, unwavering—a pilgrimage of devotion and discovery. Yet, unbeknownst to him, this journey would also lead him to the depths of his own self.

At the same time, the British, with their imperial ambitions, harbored a different agenda for India. Their strategy was cunningly pragmatic: to establish dominance over the land without provoking resistance by interfering with its deeply rooted religions. However, beneath this veneer of restraint, they nurtured an insatiable curiosity to unravel the mysteries of India, to understand its soul.Amidst this complex backdrop, Gaurakhi—a figure embodying the essence of Lord Shiva—continued on his quest. With the sacred Ganga River as his silent companion, he moved forward, heedless of time or the elements. Day and night blurred into one as he pressed onward, his spirit fueled by an unyielding determination.

The Ganga, ever-flowing and eternal, mirrored Gaurakhi's journey in its relentless course. To him, it was more than a river; it was a guiding force, a symbol of purity and persistence. As he walked along its banks, its murmuring waters seemed to whisper ancient secrets, urging him forward.Yet, Gaurakhi had no way of knowing that this journey would transform him. It was not merely a pilgrimage to honor Shiva; it was an odyssey that would bind him closer to his own essence, peeling back the layers of his being and revealing truths he had yet to comprehend. Each step he took was not just toward the Himalayas but toward the discovery of his own destiny.

Gaurakhi, a figure who seemed to embody completeness in himself.

Gaurakhi, adorned with arm ornaments, Rudraksha beads around his neck, a red bundle, a staff, a dog on his shoulder, and earrings made of bone, appeared as though he was a perfect amalgamation of Gaurakhi and Gaurakh, steadfast in his devotion to his path. His sole aim was not to falter; his intense penance was the only goal.

Seeking to quench his thirst, he sat by a well in the middle of the night, during the new moon. The darkness and the uncertainty of the path made it difficult to see, but he hoped for the dawn to continue his journey to the Himalayas. As he gazed towards a distant village, he planned to collect supplies for the journey at the first light of dawn. Settling down, he gradually drifted into a deep sleep, the cool night air bringing with it a sense of peace.

In the stillness of the night, a woman from the nearby village appeared, her face smeared with what seemed like blood. Her eyes were swollen, and she wore tattered clothing. Frantic, she stumbled towards the well, her face a picture of despair. As she reached the edge of the well and extended her hands, preparing to leap in, **Gaurakhi**, sensing her presence, intervened. His hand grasped hers, and with his powers, he was transported back a thousand years in time.

He found himself in an ancient era, where a large pot contained a beautiful young child, just 8 years old, climbing up a rope that reached towards the heavens. As the child grasped a sickle from the end of the rope, dawn broke.

It felt less like a dream and more like a vivid reality, as though the vision was trying to convey something profound to Gaurakhi. When he awoke, an overwhelming sense of exhaustion gripped him. It was as if the weight of years of illness had suddenly descended upon his body. The dream had left him drained, both physically and mentally, as if he had been fighting an unseen battle for an eternity.

His vision blurred, the world around him veiled in a misty haze. A strange heaviness settled over him, his limbs burdened with an inexplicable weariness. It felt as though time itself had twisted and turned, pulling him into its relentless tide. Every fiber of his being ached, and his body, overwhelmed by fatigue, seemed on the verge of surrender.

By now, the British had heard numerous tales about this village, whispered rumors of a dark, mysterious power residing there. However, the British dismissed these stories, attributing them to the superstitious nature of the Indian people. Skepticism clouded their minds, as they suspected that the villagers might be concocting tales of ghosts and spirits as a clever ploy to avoid labor and obligations.

The British administrators couldn't shake the feeling that these stories might be a guise—a cunning attempt by the locals to evade the Permanent Settlement system. This system, which required zamindars to pay a fixed tax, had placed a heavy burden on the people of Bengal and Bihar. The officials pondered whether these tales were merely an excuse to resist the crushing demands of the colonial tax policies, a subtle form of rebellion disguised as folklore.

At the same time, the British government sent two Christian missionaries to verify whether the deaths were due to famine or the alleged dark powers.

As the first rays of sunlight touched his Rudraksha beads, **Gaurakhi** stood up. The events of the night had forced him to reflect deeply, but he dismissed them as a dream. Nearby, an old tree bore inscriptions in Bengali, with an ancient stone beneath it. The stone had strange inscriptions on one side and **"Mandu Village"** on the other, surrounded by dried red paint and withered grass. Gaurakhnath, with a broad smile and a determined spirit, remarked:

"It's time for alms. Perhaps I'll find good fortune in Mandu and avoid needing to rest elsewhere on my journey."

Gaurakhi set out towards Mandu village. After begging for food from several homes, he was invited into one. The family, welcoming him inside,

said:

"Baba, please have something to eat. Perhaps your blessings can bring some relief to our village."

As the family conversed among themselves, they said:

"Just make sure no boy is born in any household this Amavas," one of the elders whispered, his voice heavy with dread. "If a boy is born, that dark spirit will possess him within six to seven days. And then..." He paused, his eyes darting nervously, "Lasso will return. That cursed game, that darkness, and the misfortune that comes with it... it will all begin again."

Another elder added gravely, "And by the time the next Amavas of the eighth year arrives, that boy will become part of the **Lasso Kumbh.**

Silence fell among them, their faces etched with fear and helplessness, as the weight of their words lingered in the dimly lit room.

Gaurakhi, sitting at a corner of the gathering, listens to the conversation with a great deal of amusement. Laughing heartily, he remarks, ***"Are all the people here like this? And by the way, give me more food."***

At that moment, a few elderly members of the family, showing a mixture of concern and reverence, advise him,

*"It would be wise for you to leave before evening. The **Kali Shakti** is especially potent here, so it's best if you go. We have written countless letters to the British government and tried very hard to explain that this place is under the influence of dark forces. Hunger is one thing, but there are other inexplicable occurrences as well."*

Gaurakhi, heeding their warnings, rises and returns to the well. Muttering to himself about how even alms seem questionable now and that he must set out for the night, he takes a puff from his chillum and eats a bit. Just as he starts to doze off, a strange woman dressed in bizarre attire rushes towards the well. As she stumbles and attempts to fall into it, **Gaurakhi** grabs her hand firmly. The situation unfolds as if linking the story's chain to the next chapter:

The little boy, seeing his father, asks, *"Do I look different, Papa?"*

His father, playing the flute, stops and replies, *"Yes, you look different, dear."*

A woman in the crowd, egging on the display of magic, shouts,

"Show us magic, show us magic!"

Suddenly, **Gaurakhi** feels as though he has returned from a thousand-year journey, a profound sensation overcoming him.

The moment Gaurakhi grabs the woman's hand, she collapses, and it seems as though some dark force or malevolent entity within her recognizes that he is no ordinary man, capable of reading her intentions. The dark spirit, in a bid to maintain control, exits the woman, leaving her in a state of unconsciousness.

Gaurakhi decides to take the woman to her home in the village. After visiting a few houses, he discovers that she belongs to one of them. The terrified family members express their gratitude, yet they refuse to explain further.

They insist, *"You have come from far. Purify our home and eat before you leave."*

Gaurakhi stays for the meal. After eating, he learns that the woman had given birth to a boy. This news causes the villagers to rush towards the woman's house, as the birth of a child on an *Amavasya* night is considered significant. It is believed that the child's spirit will enter the world, and many people must chant mantras to prevent any malevolent entities from interfering. The fear and urgency escalate, and the crowd of *Tantrik* (occult practitioners) gathers at the house, chanting fervently.

CHAPTER TWO

The Quest

Gaurakhi observes this commotion, feeling a sense of disquiet as he watches the villagers' growing frenzy. Despite the chaos, he decides to quietly slip away to avoid drawing attention. He notices the crowd of tantriks chanting and realizes that something is seriously wrong.

The woman writhed in excruciating pain, her cries piercing the stillness of the room. She had just given birth to a child, a moment that should have been filled with joy and relief. But the agony that followed was unbearable, far beyond the threshold of normal suffering. Her condition spoke volumes—her body convulsing, her eyes rolling back, as if retreating from the horrors within.

Marks of an eerie red hue began to appear on her skin, spreading like ominous shadows. Her face was drenched in sweat, her breaths ragged, and her eyes burned a fiery red, betraying an intensity that unnerved everyone around her. Clutching her newborn to her chest, she began to strike her hand against the floor, her wails of despair echoing through the air.

Her sorrow and pain merged into one relentless torment, as she gazed at the child with a mix of fear and anguish. The room was filled with the murmurs of those gathered around her, their voices reciting prayers and chants, an attempt to quell the storm that seemed to possess her. The chants grew louder, resonating with desperation, as if the words themselves were battling an unseen force.

The atmosphere was thick with dread, every pair of eyes locked on the suffering woman, her torment laying bare a story that none dared to speak aloud. Her pain was not merely physical; it was an enigma, a silent scream against something far more sinister than anyone could comprehend.

Gaurakhi could hardly bear to witness the woman's condition. Standing amidst the gathered crowd, his eyes were fixed on her, her agony tearing at his soul. The villagers, their faces taut with fear and urgency, turned toward Gaurakhi, gesturing for him to join them in chanting the mantras they were reciting. Their whispers and nods were clear: they believed in the power of their collective prayer to pacify whatever force was tormenting her.But to Gaurakhi, the entire scene felt strangely out of place. As a devoted follower of Lord Shiva, his faith was unwavering, yet he couldn't shake the feeling of unease creeping into his heart. The chants, the gestures, the desperate atmosphere—all of it clashed with his understanding of Shiva's divine order.

"What is happening here?" he thought, his mind racing. "Is this real? Is it all in my head? Or is it a glimpse into the harsh reality of these people's lives?" His faith clashed with the eerie strangeness of what he was witnessing, a dissonance that made him question not only the moment but also his place in it.

Gaurakhi's instincts urged him to act, to do something, but uncertainty gripped him like an unrelenting shadow. "What can I do?" he wondered. "What should I do?" His mind churned with questions, but no answers surfaced. Helplessness wrapped itself around him, a heavy shroud he could not lift.

The cries of the woman, the rhythmic cadence of the chants, and the oppressive weight of the villagers' expectations pressed down on him. Gaurakhi remained rooted to the spot, his thoughts spiraling into an abyss of doubt and confusion. In the depths of his heart, he longed to intervene, but his path forward was shrouded in uncertainty. And so, he stood there, a solitary figure in the midst of the crowd, consumed by the weight of his thoughts, struggling to reconcile his faith with the harrowing reality before him.

In his mind, he reflects on his mother's teachings:

"When you find no path through the darkness, and when the strength of a person's spirit is limited, taking the Rudraksha and closing your eyes will show you the way out. No matter how much you try, do not move it from around your neck."

Recalling this advice, **Gaurakhi** clutches the *Rudraksha* around his neck. As he holds it, the darkness around him seems to lift, revealing a path through the darkness. He sees the boy being cut into pieces and falling into a pot. Lightning cracks, and dark clouds gather as if nature itself is defying some cosmic order. The man who is performing the ritual appears to be desperate, hoping to see his son revived, but his hope seems to turn into despair.

The magic fails, and the woman falls into unconsciousness again. The man, seeing the futility of his efforts, flees. **Gaurakhi** watches this scene, feeling drained by the sheer force of the dark energy. His hands are covered in strange marks, stained with blood, and the villagers start reciting mantras with increased fervor.

Gaurakhi, overwhelmed by the dark energy, collapses.

As **Gaurakhi** lies unconscious, the villagers continue their mantras and pour Ganga water over him. Gaurakhi heard a commotion coming from a neighboring house, the sound of a woman shouting. Curious, he went over to inquire about it. Upon asking, he was told that the woman in question, a neighbor from a nearby house, was pregnant. It seemed that she was in labor, and it was expected that her child would be born either today or tomorrow. In fact, it was believed that the child might even be born on the night of the new moon.

The situation was urgent, and everyone agreed that they would need to go to her. The woman, in her condition, needed their help, and they couldn't ignore the call for assistance. The community understood the importance of coming together during such times, and **Gaurakhi**, too, knew that they must all go and offer their support to the woman in labor.

The effect of the power was dreadful, and it seemed almost impossible for Gaurakhi to survive. It wasn't going to be easy, but the villagers did not stop chanting the mantras. They lifted Gaurakhi and carried her into the dark room. Just then, an elder from the village, who had been part of the crowd, spoke up, saying, "This is the effect of Lasso. It will not go away so easily."

He continued, "Prepare the soil and bring Gaurakhi into the room. Mix the wings we collect from the insects in the fields with the soil and apply it like a paste all over his body. And, keep the chanting of the mantras continuous. If the power is willing, it might weaken, and Gaurakhi might be saved. If not, we must accept the truth that when such a power enters, no one should be allowed to touch it."

An old man came forward and asked, "Who is this? And why wasn't this explained to us earlier? It seems like someone from outside, perhaps a wandering baba, has entered our village."

One of the villagers responded, "Yes, this is Gaurakhi. He was here having a meal and was on a journey. He's from outside.

"Meanwhile, the crowd continued chanting the mantras, but Gaurakhi's body was slowly turning blue. The night of the new moon deepened, and two days later, Gaurakhi regained consciousness.

As he came to, he was terrified, his mind in disarray. His dog, which had been awake beside him for two nights, looked just as unsettled. Gaurakhi, trembling and confused, whispered, "Impossible... Such power. There's no way to answer this power. This is an incredibly strange event. It feels as though the crowd has become one, and there's a sound echoing in my head... I saw something. It's beyond my understanding. But God has spared me... I don't know what's happening. It seems this village has witnessed a lot of pain in its past."

The words hung in the air, a mix of disbelief and fear, as Gaurakhi tried to piece together what had just happened. Something in the village felt ancient, as if the wounds of the past had resurfaced, and Gaurakhi was caught in the centre of it all.

When he regains consciousness, he is greeted with expressions of gratitude from the villagers who thank him for saving their daughter from death on this ominous night. Exhausted and weak, Gaurakhi manages to gather his belongings and heads back to the well.

Upon reaching the well, he encounters two drifters from the village. They are smoking a **chillum**(Pipe) and, upon seeing **Gaurakhi,** try to flee. **Gaurakhi** catches one of them and asks, *"Why are you running away?"*

The drifter replies,

"We thought you were here to collect something from us, as we had been smoking from your chillum."

Gaurakhi, puzzled, inquires about their suspicious behavior. The drifter explains that on Amavasya nights, women come to the well, and before they fall in, they often throw away valuables or precious items. The drifters collect these items to sustain themselves. Upon noticing Gaurakhi's blood-stained hands, they become fearful.

"You seem like a thief," the drifter comments. *"Which house did you rob?"*

Gaurakhi asks for cloth to clean his hands. One drifter tears a piece of his *Dhoti* and gives it to him, saying, *"Clean yourself with this. The spirit here is obsessed with blood."* Seeing the strange marks on Gaurakhi's hands, the drifters flee in panic. Gaurakhi, weakened by the ordeal, manages to catch one and demands an explanation.

"Why are you running away?" he asks.

The drifter explains, *"This mark is no ordinary injury. It's something else entirely."*

When pressed for details, the drifter hesitates but eventually reveals, *"We have seen bloodstains on a stone in the past. It had an unusual mark similar to the one on your hand. We feared that you might be connected to that spirit, but you seem to be like us, smoking the chillum. How can a spirit consume tobacco?"*

The drifter adds, *"And one more thing – it seems the dark power here, and whatever you are, is connected to our survival."*

As the drifters leave with the *chillum,* **Gaurakhi** examines the peculiar marks on his hands. Lightning flashes and the stone reveals a similar mark as the one on his hand. To understand this mystery and resolve the riddle, Gaurakhi decides to stay another night. Exhausted, he rests beside the stone, determined to uncover its connection to the marks on his hands.The next morning, as Gaurakhi examines the stone and its markings, two British agents arrive in the village, sent by the Church to investigate the truth of the dark phenomena. The agents, representatives of the British government, have been dispatched as part of the Regulating Act of 1773, tasked with overseeing British interests in Bengal and the East India Company's operations.

The British agents, observing **Gaurakhi's** strange attire and actions, approach him.

First Britisher: "Who is this foul-smelling thing, this filthy-looking person?"

Second Britisher: *"I think he might be uncovering some information here."*

First Britisher: *"Who are you?"*

(Gaurakhi sits silently, completely ignoring the words of the white-skinned people.)

Second Britisher: "I think, *He seems to be involved in occult activities.*"

First Britisher: *"The way he is dressed, and his actions... Is he the one?"*

Second Britisher : Hope so!

First Brtitisher : "It seems like he is recognizing these letters. I think he might know Sanskrit."

*(**Gaurakhi,** who remains silent. They call for additional British officers to assist in detaining him, suspecting him of being involved in the supernatural events in the village. **Gaurakhi** offers to read the inscriptions, which are in Sanskrit, and the agents, intrigued, realize his potential value).*

First Britisher: *"Sanskrit? Really?"*

Second Britisher: *"Oh, wonderful! He can be our translator."*

First Britisher: *"Indeed! He is a valuable asset."*

Gaurakhi responds, *"I can read what is written, and even what is not written."*

The British agents, recognizing Gaurakhi's potential, take him with them, contemplating how his knowledge of Sanskrit and the occult could serve their interests.

As they depart, the agents discuss among themselves:

Second Britisher: *"Sanskrit is a source of knowledge and money. He is like a blank cheque for us."*

First Britisher:*"Absolutely! He will be invaluable to us."*

And so, **Gaurakhi** is drawn into a new chapter of his journey, marked by political intrigue and the quest for deeper understanding of the dark forces that bind the village and its mysterious stone.

It was an era of translation when numerous texts were being translated into English. During this period, important works like the **Geeta, Mahabharata, Kalidasa's** epics, and many other great literary pieces were being translated. In such a time, **Warren Hastings** and the English scholars accompanying him studied Sanskrit and translated it. Amidst this, how could they overlook **Gaurakhnath?**

During this time, the **Nalanda University**, established by **Kumaragupta** and later destroyed by **Bakhtiyar Khilji**, was still remembered. It is said that books burned for three months, but some were partially saved. To rule India, understanding its history through these books was crucial. At the same time, this was a kind of intellectual theft. **Gaurakhnath,** who was brought to the specialists brought by Hastings, had to decipher these texts. The scholars said:

First Scholar:

"Look, if you really decipher it, we will surely spare you. Otherwise, you will have to face our Governor General."

If **Gaurakhnath** could decipher the texts, it would show his proficiency; otherwise, he would be accused of causing the disturbances in the village and be blamed by the East India Company.

Second Scholar: *"You are allotted a bandwidth of seven days. By then, decipher it and prove to us that you have the power to do so."*When **Gaurakhi** began to study the books brought from Nalanda, he was told that they would return after a week. Until then, he had to understand and explain them.

Gaurakhi was deeply engrossed in thought, surrounded by questions. Among the burnt books, he picked up one hoping to find some valuable information. Over the next 2-3 days, he spent time by the books, remembering his guru and reflecting deeply.

Two or three days had passed, and while Gaurakhi's condition was gradually improving, the toll on his body remained evident. The spiritual possession had left him physically weakened, his strength sapped as though drained by an unseen force. Each passing night, however, brought vivid dreams that seemed to guide and heal him in some inexplicable way. These dreams were not mere fragments of his subconscious but felt like glimpses into a realm that transcended reality.

In his dreams, Gaurakhi often saw his mother, her face radiating warmth and reassurance. At other times, he envisioned the powers bestowed upon him by his guru, the teachings and blessings that once made him feel invincible. Yet amidst these comforting visions, there lingered a strange disturbance within his mind. It was as if a growing turbulence was taking shape, compelling him to confront something far beyond his understanding. Within these visions, a peculiar form began to emerge—a devotee of Shiva or perhaps another Gaurakhi, incomplete yet hauntingly familiar.

The dream sharpened each night, its clarity intensifying with an unsettling precision. It no longer felt like a dream but rather an event edging closer to reality, as though the boundaries between the two were dissolving. Gaurakhi couldn't shake the sense that this vision was drawing him toward something inevitable, something profoundly significant.

On the fifth day, while studying a collection of ancient texts, Gaurakhi stumbled upon a book unlike any he had seen before. Its weathered cover bore enigmatic symbols and markings, their meaning shrouded in mystery. Though faded and indistinct, the symbols seemed oddly familiar. With a growing sense of unease, Gaurakhi's gaze lingered on the patterns, realizing they bore a striking resemblance to the markings on his own hands. The discovery sent a shiver through him, as if the book and the dreams were intricately connected, pulling him into a web of destiny he had yet to unravel.

He came across a book that had a particular mark similar to one on his hand. He took this book to read. Although some pages were burned, some remained intact. As he read, he found a reference to a tantric—**Vetalbhadra.**

Vetalbhadra:

Vetalbhadra was one of Chandragupta II's nine gems. He had mastered the dark arts, and Chandragupta did not want his efforts to create any problems in the kingdom. Vetalbhadra had learned the art of reversing the life cycle, essentially bringing the dead back to life and controlling the structure of nature. This dark magic was intended to show

Chandragupta his position among the nine gems.

To perform this magic, **Vetalbhadra** chose a young boy from a noble family, invoking mantras and applying ash to bind him with his soul.

CHAPTER THREE

The Magic

The magic involved:

A large pot made of ashes from the cremation ground was used, which was heated over the pyre. In this pot, a rope was dipped. A thick liquid, made from coconut husks, was added. Chanting mantras, the boy, naked, was placed on this rope, which was performed during the new moon night. Before 3 AM, which was considered the dominion of demonic forces, the boy would start cutting his own body under the magician's direction. The cut pieces would be placed in the pot, and then through mantra chanting, the body would be transformed back into a living form. This was a way to triumph over death.

When Chandragupta learned about this, he warned **Vetalbhadra**, but fate had its own plans. **Vetalbhadra's** years of hard work could not go in vain. He completed the magic, noting an unusual occurrence in the book.

As **Gaurakhnath** flipped through the pages, he read:

During the performance of this magic, a demonic force learned its secret.

"I made the mistake of understanding the separation between the soul and body but forgot other souls. One of them entered me, and though I tried to stop it with magic, it was too late. The soul started to enter me, and though

I tried to halt it with all my powers, my body and mental balance deteriorated. I inscribed the mantra that I used to stop it on every tree and stone. Later, the villagers began to demand to see the magic during the new moon. The only way to survive was the mantra. After this calamity, the Gupta dynasty expelled me from the village. "

As Gaurakhi delved deeper into the mysticism of the Gupta dynasty, he began to connect its secrets to the cryptic dreams that had been plaguing his nights. The parallels were undeniable, and his thoughts returned to the peculiar sensation he had experienced when he touched the afflicted woman. It felt as though he had brushed against the remnants of the same arcane power. Vetalbhadra—the name lingered in his mind, its weight growing heavier with each passing day. The notion that another spirit had intruded into the woman's body gnawed at him, and the question of why the ritual had failed haunted his every thought.

Gaurakhi realized that the answers he sought could only be found at Kamakhya, the temple that served as a gateway to the knowledge of such esoteric practices. Vetalbhadra, being a master of Tantric rituals, was intricately linked to Kamakhya's mysteries. But Gaurakhi faced a dilemma: how could he convince the British officials to grant him passage to the temple? He knew they would require a compelling justification, and he would need to tread carefully.

Six days passed, and the moment Gaurakhi had been waiting for finally arrived. Two British officers approached him, their faces stern and unreadable. One of them spoke in a clipped tone, "Show us what you've accomplished in these days. It's time to see if you truly understand Sanskrit or if your claims were empty boasts. And mark my words, Gaurakhi, if you've done nothing or try to make excuses, the consequences will be severe. We'll ensure your name is linked to all the strange happenings in this village. You know the punishment Governor-General will mete out for that."

Gaurakhi listened silently, his expression impassive, even as tension coiled in his chest. He waited until the officer finished speaking before stepping forward. "There is one book I've studied extensively," he began, gesturing toward a tome he had placed nearby. "It contains crucial information about the practices and rituals linked to the mysteries of this village. I believe I've uncovered something significant."

The officers exchanged a glance, visibly pleased with his progress. Encouraged by their reaction, Gaurakhi continued, "In my research, I discovered an ancient text tied to dark magic. However, to fully comprehend its contents, I need access to the Kamakhya temple. That temple is the only place where such mystical knowledge can be unraveled. Without going there, I fear the truth behind what's happening in this village will remain out of reach."

The officers conferred in hushed voices, debating the plausibility of his request. After a moment, they nodded. "Very well," one of them said. "We'll present your request to the Governor-General. But understand this, Gaurakhi: any information you uncover at Kamakhya must first be reported to us. You will not share it with anyone else before we have reviewed it."

Gaurakhi bowed his head in agreement, hiding the flicker of triumph in his eyes. He had taken the first step toward his goal.

Two days later, the officers returned with news. "The Governor-General has granted permission," one of them announced. "You are to accompany us to Kamakhya. But remember, any findings will be reported to him directly, and only then will you be allowed to walk free."

"Understood," Gaurakhi replied with measured calm.

"Good," the officer said, motioning toward the waiting carriage. "Then let us depart for Kamakhya."

The English sent him to **Kamakhya** with four soldiers.

Gaurakhi reached **Kamakhya** Temple, which was renowned for stopping dark forces and was supreme in tantric practices. **Kamakhya** is believed to protect humans from the realms of heaven and hell. It is said to be the gate where even the damned souls could be saved. **Gaurakhi** came to uncover the secret of the magic at this temple. As he saw the grandeur of the temple, tears flowed from his eyes.

At night, the soldiers kept watch, and **Gaurakhi** fell asleep inside the temple. Night is said to be the precursor to light. There were untold paths. Gaurakhi had finally arrived at Kamakhya, but he was unsure of what to do next. The weight of the British government's expectations loomed heavily over him, along with his own burning questions that sought answers. Determined to make progress, Gaurakhi began his work by compiling a meticulous list of tantriks associated with the temple throughout different periods of history. It was an exhaustive task that consumed more than a week of his time. Once the list was complete, he started arranging the names chronologically, hoping to uncover some vital clue.

Despite his thorough efforts, there came a point where Gaurakhi's research hit a wall. No matter how many times he revisited the names or how deeply he probed into each entry, there were gaps in the records. Certain tantriks seemed to have vanished from history, leaving no trace behind. Frustration grew as days passed with no significant breakthrough. Gaurakhi, overwhelmed by the enormity of his task and the mysterious dead ends, sat down heavily, contemplating his next steps.

However, something unusual had been happening to him ever since he set foot in Kamakhya. Every night, vivid dreams enveloped him, the kind he could not shake even after waking. These dreams seemed to build upon themselves, becoming increasingly clearer with each passing night. In these dreams, Gaurakhi found himself creating a peculiar shape, a divine symbol meant to appease Lord Shiva. But there was something... or someone... different within the dreams. It was as if another version of himself, a more enlightened and spiritually adept Gaurakhi, was guiding him. This figure chanted mantras with crystal-clear clarity, and the words resonated deeply in Gaurakhi's consciousness.

Though the dreams offered him fragments of insight, they also left him with a mounting sense of confusion. What were they trying to tell him? Why did they feel both familiar and foreign? Seeking clarity, Gaurakhi returned to his list of tantriks. This time, he scrutinized every detail with fresh determination. As his eyes scanned the names, he realized something startling—Vetalbhadra, the tantrik who had been pivotal in earlier events, was conspicuously absent from the records.

The realization struck him like lightning. It was Vetalbhadra—the elusive figure missing from the list—who held the answers he sought. Gaurakhi's instincts told him that Vetalbhadra was the key to unraveling the mysteries surrounding Kamakhya and his own visions. Now, more determined than ever, he resolved to uncover the truth about Vetalbhadra, no matter what it took.

Despite **Gaurakhi's** best efforts, he couldn't find the path. Exhausted and with divine light descending upon him, **Gaurakhi** encountered the divine form of **Gaurakhnath.**

Gaurakhnath Dev:

"**Gaurakhnath**, rise. You have been facing this dilemma since childhood. Today, I reveal a truth to you. You are a part of me. Your destiny brought you here. Listen to me."

"I am **Gaurakhnath**. My devotion to my guru **Matyasendra** was boundless. I could not live without him. My devotion elevated me in his eyes, but **Matyasendra** was concerned that my unwavering love might lead to envy. He advised me to practice austerity. After 14 years of penance on the mountains, when I returned to meet my guru, I found another disciple in the cave. Despite my repeated inquiries, I was told the guru was not inside. I forced my way into the cave and found that my guru was not there. Afterward, I used my powers and knowledge gained from my austerity to find out what had happened to my guru. This misuse of power is known as dark magic. When I finally reached my guru, he was very displeased. For the trial he had prepared me for, I had failed. To protect myself from envy and anger, he sentenced me to another 14 years of penance. Unable to bear this, I begged him to let me complete a difficult posture. He agreed and gave me a challenging one."

"Listen, Gaurakhi, my descendant, your presence here and your efforts are not in vain. Your path is here in this temple."

"Create what I made, and whatever I couldn't create, you will. There is a remarkable posture within you, similar to my childhood posture."

Waking up from the dream , **Gaurakhi** pondered deeply and realized the meaning of the divine command. He began creating the posture.

Two or three days had passed, yet Gaurakhnath still couldn't understand in which form he should shape his body to find the path. Meanwhile, the British began to think that he might be a fraud—someone who knew nothing. But they were still reluctant to dismiss him entirely. They wanted to wait a little longer, uncertain whether their assumptions about him might be wrong.

One day, they approached him with a mocking tone, eager to humiliate him. "It's been more than two months," they said. "And you still haven't figured anything out. You're a fraud! You've dragged us here to this Kamakhya Temple for no reason."

"We'll give you one or two more days, Gaurakhi. If you don't show us something by then, we'll throw you out like we did the others. Everyone will think you died from starvation."

Gaurakhi fixed them with a fierce, burning stare. The British, unsettled by the intensity of his gaze, struck him across the back with a whip. "Lower your eyes," they commanded. "We are doing you a favor by helping people like you. Don't forget that."

Despite working on it for an hour, he couldn't complete it. Frustrated, he sat down as he did in his childhood. **Gaurakhi** had always wanted to leave home, and despite repeated attempts to convince his mother, he never relented. He believed there was something beyond the ordinary. His mother, thinking it was dark magic, had shown him to many sages with no solution. Eventually, when frustrated, she would leave him to his own devices, and when he did something unusual, she would leave him be.

Finally, Gaurakhi managed to recreate the form that had been appearing in his dreams, becoming clearer and closer each night. This was the very form once designed by Gaurakhnath Dev himself when he had been sent back after completing 14 years of penance. However, this form had a deeper significance—it was not just a punishment imposed by his guru, Matsyendra, but a path to unlock divine knowledge. Matsyendra had instructed Gaurakhnath to adopt this form and engage in unwavering devotion for another 14 years as both penance and preparation.

The form was an intricate technique, a key to unlocking the gateways of wisdom. By adopting this posture, any seeker of knowledge could channel their energies to discover their destined path. For days, Gaurakhi had been haunted by visions of this very form, urging him toward something greater. The dreams were guiding him because he, too, was on a quest—for answers, for understanding, for the way forward.

In his dream that fateful night, Gaurakhi found himself embodying the form. Balancing on the tip of his right big toe, he folded his left leg inward and sat upon it mid-air. His hands stretched upward, palms open to the heavens. As he began to chant, the sound of his mantras resonated with the primal forces around him. The winds picked up in a fierce gale, howling through the trees and corridors of the Kamakhya temple.

The bells in the temple rang out violently, their clangs echoing like thunder in the storm. The ground beneath seemed to hum with energy as though the earth itself was responding to Gaurakhi's invocation. The atmosphere was electric, a blend of chaos and harmony, a testament to the power of the form and the truths it unlocked.

In that moment, Gaurakhi understood why this form had called to him. It was not merely a pose but a manifestation of surrender, discipline, and divine connection. It was the bridge between mortal comprehension and the infinite realms of divine knowledge. The answer he sought was near, and yet the mystery deepened, for this was only the beginning of the revelations that awaited him.

Vetalbhadra's voice began to echo in Gaurakhi's ears, growing louder and more intense with every passing moment. It wasn't just a sound—it was a force, pulling him toward a path he had never seen before. In his mind's eye, he saw an ancient temple, secluded in a forgotten corner of the village, its walls painted a faded crimson and marked with black, ominous symbols. A strange, spiritual energy seemed to radiate from it, as though something—or someone—had been waiting there for an eternity. A flicker of light in the darkness, a beckoning call, stirred within him. The path was clear, illuminated by the vision Gaurakhi had unlocked after forming the sacred posture.

The wind howled, bending the tall grasses in the direction of the temple. Thunder cracked across the sky, and the air grew dense with a foreboding energy. Gaurakhi felt an overwhelming pull, as though the very elements were urging him forward. But the intensity of the experience became too much for him to bear. The brilliance of the posture's power overwhelmed his senses, and his body convulsed before he collapsed to the ground, unconscious. His body trembled violently, and the sound of his fall echoed through the chamber, reaching the British guards stationed outside.

Alarmed, the guards rushed in, their boots clattering against the stone floors. The sight before them was unsettling—Gaurakhi's pale, shivering form lay sprawled across the ground, his breathing shallow and labored. A wave of panic swept over the men. If Gaurakhi died here, they knew they would face the wrath of their officers, perhaps even the Governor-General himself. How would they explain his death? What reason could they give?

The East India Company had sworn an unspoken oath—they were here to exploit India's resources, not interfere in its religion or spirituality. But now, standing over Gaurakhi's seemingly lifeless body, the guards feared they had inadvertently crossed that line. Desperate to avoid being implicated, they carried Gaurakhi's body into the dense jungle and left him there, hoping nature would claim what they no longer wanted responsibility for.

By dawn, they returned to their posts, telling anyone who asked that Gaurakhi had fled during the night. When word of this reached the General, he dismissed it with barely a thought. "Find him," he ordered curtly, "but do not waste your time. If he cannot be found, seek others with the same skills. We need men who can understand Sanskrit if we are to comprehend these people's texts. To rule this land, we must first understand it."

Relieved at the General's dismissal of the matter, the guards felt a weight lifted from their shoulders. Their mistake had been forgotten, and they turned their attention to finding other scholars who could assist the British Empire in its insidious plans.

Meanwhile, Gaurakhi stirred where the guards had left him, faint sunlight filtering through the thick canopy above. Disoriented, he tried to piece together his fragmented memories. Had everything he experienced been real? Or was it all just another vivid dream? The visions of the temple, the storm, the sacred posture—had any of it truly happened, or was it all in his mind? Slowly, as his strength returned, he recalled the events leading up to his collapse and resolved to seek the truth.

Determined, Gaurakhi gathered his thoughts and set out to find the temple he had seen in his vision. The path was unclear, and doubt lingered in his mind. Was this temple real? Or was it merely an illusion? He stopped to ask villagers about it, but most could only offer blank stares or dismissive shrugs. Finally, an elderly woman, her face weathered by time, spoke up.

"Yes, Baba," she said, her voice trembling with age. "There was once such a temple. My great-grandfather used to speak of it in his stories. They called it the Crimson-Black Temple, and it is now nothing but ruins. No one dares go there. It is overrun by snakes and scorpions. The place is cursed."

She paused, her cataract-clouded eyes narrowing as she regarded Gaurakhi. "If you value your life, do not go there. The path you are walking now will lead you to it in one or two kilometers. But it is nightfall. Do not go. Wait until the light of day."

Gaurakhi listened to her warning but felt the pull of his vision stronger than ever. He nodded politely, but his heart was already set. If the answers he sought lay within that ruined temple, he would face whatever darkness awaited him.Gaurakhi knew he had to solve the mystery. Ignoring all fears and warnings, he pressed forward along the path. The night deepened around him, the forest alive with the distant sounds of nocturnal creatures. When exhaustion finally caught up with him, he decided to rest. Sitting down under a tree, he pulled some food from his satchel. First, he fed his loyal dog, who wagged its tail eagerly, and then he ate what little remained.

Nearby, a field of dried chickpea plants caught his eye. He gathered some of the stalks, lit a small fire, and roasted the pods over the flames, savoring the simple warmth and nourishment. Once his stomach was full, Gaurakhi stoked the fire higher, ensuring it would burn brightly through the night and keep wild animals at bay. He lay down near its warmth, listening to the crackle of the flames as sleep overtook him.

Time moved on, indifferent to his quest, and the pale light of dawn soon broke through the canopy of trees. Gaurakhi woke, groggy but resolute. He washed his face in a nearby stream, the cold water refreshing him. His dog danced around him playfully, its wagging tail a brief reminder of joy amid the heaviness of his mission. Gaurakhi knelt, laughing as he played with the creature for a few precious moments, letting the weight of his thoughts lift just slightly.

But duty called. As he walked a few paces further in search of water, his eyes fell upon a reflection in the stillness of a nearby pond—a crimson structure, weathered and ancient, its edges sharp against the misty morning air. Gaurakhi froze, his heart racing. Could it be the temple from his vision? He turned his gaze toward the horizon and saw another crumbling ruin just behind him. Its stones were darkened with age, ivy creeping through the cracks, as though time itself had forgotten it.

Without hesitation, Gaurakhi ran toward the ruins. His breath quickened as he reached the crumbled walls, his hands brushing against their rough, cold surface. Something about the place felt alive, as though the air around it pulsed with an unseen energy. On one of the walls, he noticed peculiar markings—ancient Sanskrit, painted in black, fragmented and partially obscured. The script was unfamiliar, twisted and uneven, as though written in haste or perhaps by a trembling hand.

Gaurakhi traced the words with his fingers, his eyes scanning the text. These weren't ordinary inscriptions—they were mantras. He began to read, his voice low and steady, the ancient syllables reverberating through the ruins as if they had been waiting for centuries to be spoken once more.

'*Swarnat Vijaya Vidmahe Sula Hastaya Dhimahi Tanno Kala Bhairavaya Prachodaya.*'

This mantra was intended to counteract the dark magic and break the curse. The book revealed that the curse was linked to the soul, and the only way to counter it was through a powerful and pure form of dark magic. The key was to understand and use the magic correctly, as described."

Gaurakhi's journey was not only about overcoming a curse but also about mastering the ancient arts and discovering his own divine potential.

As Gaurakhi explored the ruins, he stumbled upon something extraordinary. In a small, concealed alcove within the crumbling structure, he found thin wooden planks stacked haphazardly, their surfaces etched with intricate markings. Carefully lifting one of the planks, he realized they weren't ordinary carvings but inscriptions—ancient writings meticulously etched into the wood, as though someone had gone to great lengths to preserve a long-forgotten story.Gaurakhi's heart raced as he examined the fragile planks. The inscriptions were written in a script so archaic and complex that even he, well-versed in Sanskrit, struggled to decipher them fully. Slowly, he pieced together fragments of the text. It wasn't just a story; it was history—hidden chapters of the past, secrets buried too deep for ordinary historians to unearth.

As he read further, the words seemed to echo in his mind, almost as though they carried their own voice: "This is the history unseen by scholars, the truth hidden in the folds of time. But who can escape me? I am Time itself."

The declaration sent chills down Gaurakhi's spine. It was as if Time, in its infinite wisdom, had decided to reveal this forgotten truth to him. The planks unveiled events long erased from the collective memory of humankind, their revelations profound and unsettling. This was no ordinary history; it was a secret that defied the very narrative taught by the world.

Gaurakhi felt a strange connection to the writings, as if they were meant for him and him alone. With each plank, the story became clearer, illuminating a hidden facet of existence that had been deliberately obscured. He gently set the planks down, careful not to damage the fragile relics, and sat back to process what he had uncovered.

It was a moment of revelation and awe—a bridge between the past and the present, illuminated by the unyielding march of time. Whatever lay ahead, Gaurakhi knew one thing for certain: this discovery would change everything.

In the final plank, it is written:

"My body is reaching its end; I cannot endure this power any longer. Only ashes will be able to bear it. The warmth of the ashes will protect me from that dark force."

Gaurakhi sat inside the crimson-black temple, pondering the path forward and the nature of the way out. His hands were aching and burning. A dog was licking him. Suddenly, **Gaurakhi** remembered a sign and thought:

"This mark—this mark—if the soul did not want me to know all this, why the mark? The mark on the hand—it means

someone wanted to tell me. Who left this mark? What was it?"

When Gaurakhi had aided the pregnant woman in Munda village—helping her bring a child into the world and liberating her from the clutches of a restless spirit—he had noticed something peculiar. As he grasped her hand in the ritual, an unusual mark appeared on his palm. It wasn't just any mark; it felt as though it carried a message, a cryptic symbol etched into his flesh, left behind by the very spirit he had freed.

At first, Gaurakhi dismissed it as an illusion, perhaps a trick of his weary mind. But as time passed, the mark remained, growing clearer and more profound with each passing day. It was as if the spirit had imprinted something upon him, trying to communicate a truth beyond words. The symbol lingered, pulsing faintly as though alive, and with it came an unshakable sense of urgency. It was calling to him.

Despite his deep knowledge of rituals, chants, and ancient texts, Gaurakhi found himself unable to decipher the mark. Every attempt to understand its meaning led him to the same conclusion: this was no ordinary sign. It was tied to the very essence of the restless soul he had encountered in Munda village. The realization struck him like a flash of lightning—if he were to uncover the truth, he would need to return to the source. He would have to face the spirit once more.

The decision weighed heavily on him. Munda village had been a place of turmoil, the air thick with the echoes of unresolved anguish. Yet, he knew he couldn't ignore the pull of the mark. Its significance gnawed at him relentlessly, and with every beat of his heart, the call grew stronger. He had no choice; the path was clear.

Determined, Gaurakhi packed his modest belongings, ensuring he carried enough provisions for the journey. He checked his satchel for the tools of his trade: a few essential texts, sacred threads, and the protective charms he always kept close. As he prepared to leave, his faithful dog wagged its tail enthusiastically, sensing an adventure ahead.Gaurakhi stepped onto the winding road, the first light of dawn casting a golden glow over the landscape. The journey to Munda village would be long, and the weight of the unknown pressed heavily on his shoulders. Yet, he walked with purpose, driven by the need to uncover the truth hidden within the mark on his hand.

The road stretched endlessly before him, the quiet hum of nature his only companion. As he traversed the familiar path, Gaurakhi's mind raced with questions. Why had the spirit chosen him? What message did the mark hold? And more importantly, what awaited him in Munda village? These thoughts consumed him, but he knew one thing for certain—answers lay ahead, and he was ready to face whatever awaited him in the shadows of the unknown.

Gaurakhi quickly entered the village. The woman possessed by the soul, somewhere, held the key to this mystery. When he arrived at her house, her condition was still very delicate. The villagers tried to prevent **Gaurakhi** from touching her, but he reassured them that he would free the entire village from this curse. Gaurakhi knew with unwavering certainty that if he were to summon the spirit once more, he would need to wait for the night of Amavasya. It was a night of profound power, when the veil between the realms of the living and the dead grew thin, and restless souls could be drawn forth. The days seemed to crawl as he waited, each one stretching endlessly as his anticipation grew. But finally, the night of the new moon arrived.

The village buzzed with activity as the darkness descended. Clay lamps glowed softly, their flickering flames casting golden halos in the cool night air. It was as though another festival of light had descended upon the land, the villagers celebrating with quiet reverence. For most, it was an evening of tradition and ritual. But for Gaurakhi, the night carried a far graver purpose.Unbothered by the festivities around him, Gaurakhi positioned himself beside the woman who had once been a vessel for the spirit. Her face was drawn, her features tired as though the events of her ordeal still lingered in her very bones. She sat silently, a reluctant participant in Gaurakhi's pursuit of answers.

The hours dragged on as Gaurakhi attempted to summon the spirit. He chanted ancient mantras, lit sacred incense, and performed every ritual in his arsenal. But no matter how many times he tried, the spirit would not come. The woman, who had once been a home for the restless entity, remained untouched by its presence. It was as though the spirit itself resisted him, defying every effort he made.Frustration crept into Gaurakhi's mind as he pondered the enigma before him. The spirit had lived within this woman for eight long years, tethered to her body until he had intervened. Why wouldn't it return now? He realized that the spirit's bond to the woman was not one of choice but of necessity. For eight years, her body had been its sanctuary, its prison—until Gaurakhi had forced it to depart. To call it back, he would need to offer something irresistible.

Closing his eyes, Gaurakhi stilled his thoughts and began to meditate. He delved deep into his mind, searching for the thread that would pull the spirit from its hiding place. Slowly, an idea began to form. The spirit was bound by its desires, its longing for a vessel to inhabit. If he could awaken that longing, if he could tempt it with the promise of a return, perhaps it would come.

Summoning all his focus, Gaurakhi began to weave a spiritual net, baited with the allure of its former home. He spoke softly, coaxing the spirit with his words, offering it what it craved most. The air grew heavy, and a cold wind stirred around them. The woman shuddered as a low, guttural sound began to rise from her throat.

"Lasso... lasso..." The word escaped her lips, her voice unnaturally deep and resonant. The sound reverberated in the stillness, sending chills down Gaurakhi's spine. He watched as her body tensed, her fingers curling as though grasping at something unseen. The spirit had returned.

Gaurakhi held his breath as he observed the transformation, the lines of reality blurring before his eyes. The woman was no longer entirely herself. The spirit's presence had taken hold, and its voice carried the weight of centuries. For the first time, Gaurakhi felt the enormity of what he had unleashed—and he braced himself for the truths it might reveal.

Finally, Gaurakhi forged a connection with the spirit, his consciousness merging with its restless energy. It was as if a window to the past had opened before his eyes, allowing him to witness events long buried by the sands of time. His body began to betray him, his skin turning a deep shade of blue as though the spirit's energy was draining the very life from him. Yet, even as his strength waned, his resolve remained unshaken.

Before embarking on this perilous ritual, Gaurakhi had gathered the villagers and spoken with unflinching determination. "No matter what happens, even if I die in the midst of this ritual, none of you shall interfere. This is my path, my karma, and I have the right to walk it to its end. If I survive, perhaps I will be able to do something meaningful for all of you. But if not, let it be known that I chose this fate."

The villagers, though frightened, had agreed to his terms. Their fear was palpable, their eyes filled with both dread and hope as they watched from a distance. Some prayed silently for his safety, while others prepared themselves for the worst. But none dared step forward to defy his wishes.

As the ritual progressed, Gaurakhi's body grew weaker. His breaths came in shallow gasps, and the once-strong frame of the man now seemed fragile, almost ghostly. Yet his mind remained steadfast, guided by the spirit's force. He began to see through its eyes, to experience memories not his own. It was a torrent of images and sensations, chaotic and vivid, pulling him deeper into the unknown.

Suddenly, the scene shifted. Gaurakhi found himself standing amidst a village cloaked in an eerie fog. The air was thick with despair, and the muffled cries of people echoed in the distance. He saw a woman, her face familiar yet distant—a shadow of the very spirit he had summoned. She stood at the edge of a riverbank, clutching something close to her chest, her body trembling with sorrow.

The spirit's memories surged forward, and Gaurakhi's vision blurred as he was drawn deeper into its torment. He saw betrayal, loss, and an unrelenting hunger for justice. These emotions washed over him like a storm, their intensity threatening to drown him. His body convulsed, and he collapsed to the ground, the energy of the spirit overwhelming his physical form.From the corner of his fading consciousness, Gaurakhi could hear the panicked whispers of the villagers. They had kept their promise not to interfere, but their fear for his life was palpable. Some knelt in prayer, others clutched their children tightly, shielding them from the sight of his suffering.

As his body trembled and his mind spiraled into darkness, Gaurakhi felt a strange calm begin to settle over him. The spirit's energy, once wild and unrestrained, now seemed to envelop him in a protective embrace. Through the haze, a single, resounding truth began to emerge—a truth buried deep within the memories of the spirit and tied to the destiny of his own journey.

Gaurakhi's body was failing, but his spirit burned brighter than ever. This was no longer just a ritual. It was a reckoning—a confrontation with the past that held the key to the future. As the visions continued to unfold, Gaurakhi braced himself for the revelations that would change everything. Gaurakhi sees :

Madhav sat by the dim firelight, his hands trembling as he held the frail body of his young son, in his arms. The boy's skin had turned a terrifying shade of black, his breaths shallow and labored. It was Amavasya again—the night of the new moon, the night that seemed to bring nothing but ruin into Madhav's life. Earlier that evening, Gayatri, his wife, had once again been overtaken by the presence that haunted her for years. Possessed, her voice had taken on an unnatural timbre, a deep and chilling resonance as she repeated the words like a mantra: **"Madhav, lasso dikhao. Lasso! Lasso!"**

Madhav's jaw clenched as he tried to reason with her, his voice filled with desperation. "Gayatri, I cannot do this! We lost our firstborn, Rudra, eight years ago on this very night. You think I'll risk everything again for some cursed ritual? I won't lose our second child too. I won't lose you either. You mean more to me than any of this!"

But Gayatri, her mind clouded by the spirit's influence, had refused to relent. Her eyes burned with an otherworldly light, and her words became more frantic. "Madhav, you don't understand! Show the lasso! Rudra needs it! He's waiting! He's calling!"Madhav turned his back on her pleas, his focus solely on the child lying on the cot behind him. Rudra was his anchor, his hope, his everything. "No,"Madhav said firmly, z"this family has suffered enough. I will not invoke that cursed magic. Never again."

As the night deepened, Gayatri, overcome by her possession, stormed out of the house. Madhav, too consumed with tending to Rudra's ailing health, did not stop her. He assumed, as he always did, that she would return to her parents' house, as was her habit whenever anger consumed her.

The next few hours passed in agony. Rudra's condition worsened with every moment. His breathing became shallow, his limbs stiffened, and finally, with one last shuddering gasp, the child lay still. Madhav cradled his son, his body shaking with grief. By the time the sun rose, Madhav's heart had shattered into a thousand pieces. He rushed to Gayatri's parents' house, screaming her name. "Gayatri! Gayatri! Forgive me! I couldn't save him—our second child is gone too! I couldn't save Rudra! Please, come back to me!"

But it wasn't Gayatri who emerged from the house. Her elderly parents stepped out instead, their faces etched with sorrow and resignation. Her father gently guided Madhav to a seat, his voice calm yet heavy with emotion. "Madhav, sit down. Compose yourself. We've all suffered enough."

Madhav shook his head violently, tears streaming down his face. "I failed her! I failed Rudra! Why did she leave?

Why did she make me choose between her and our son?!"Madhav's body was drenched in Rudra's blood, his trembling hands clutching the fabric of his tunic. His face was ashen, his voice faltering as he muttered into the silence, "Gayatri... come out. Please, come out."

Gayatri's parents, standing nearby, exchanged worried glances. Her father stepped forward hesitantly. "Madhav," he said carefully, "Gayatri should be with you. Why would she come here? She hasn't been home in years."

Madhav turned to them, his eyes wild with despair. "Lasso... Kumbh..."he whispered hoarsely. Then, as if a dam had burst, his words poured out in agony. "She was right. Gayatri told me to show her the lasso, and I didn't listen. If only I had, this wouldn't have happened. This black magic has taken everything from me. Rudra is gone, and now... I couldn't even save Gayatri."

Gayatri's parents froze, their expressions shifting from confusion to terror. Their faces paled as the weight of Madhav's words settled over them. They knew this day would come—they had known for years. Rudra had turned eight, and Vetalbhadra's prophecy had begun to unravel before their eyes.

Without another word, the three of them hurried to the old well on the outskirts of the village. The well was infamous, shrouded in dark tales of despair and death. It was said that women, unable to bear their grief or escape the cursed fate tied to their homes, would leap into its depths to end their suffering.

As they approached the well, the eerie silence was broken by murmured conversations among a group of villagers gathered nearby.

"Just a day or two ago,"one man said, lowering his voice, "a woman jumped into this well. They say it was Gayatri."

Another nodded solemnly. "She used to come here every night, crying and drawing strange symbols on a stone by the well."

Madhav's heart clenched as he listened, his mind racing.

"She'd sit here for hours," another villager added, "muttering the same word over and over—'lasso.' People tried to talk to her, but she wouldn't say much. Then one night... she was gone. Disappeared into the well."

Madhav fell to his knees at the edge of the well, his bloodied hands gripping the rough stones as tears streamed down his face. "Gayatri... why?" he whispered, his voice breaking. "Why didn't you let me save you? Why didn't you tell me?"

Unseen by those in the present, Gaurakhi stood silently, watching the tragic scene unfold before him. The weight of Madhav's despair hung heavy in the air, and the echoes of his cries seemed to pierce Gaurakhi's very soul. In the present, Gaurakhi's body began to weaken, his hands trembling and his veins throbbing with the strain of the visions. But despite the physical toll, his resolve was unshaken. He had to see more. He had to understand the truth behind the cursed well, the prophecy, and the tragic bond between Madhav, Gayatri, and their lost child, Rudra.

Gayatri's mother knelt beside him, her own eyes glistening with unshed tears. "Madhav, you've suffered, yes. But do you think we haven't? Gayatri was our daughter. Losing her broke us just as much as it broke you. But Rudra—he was her last connection to this world, her final gift. And now he's gone too."

The words struck Madhav like a dagger. His mind reeled with memories of the love and loss that defined his life with Gayatri. He had believed he could outlast the curse, outmaneuver the spirit that haunted their lives. But now, staring into the empty void where his family once stood, he realized the cost of his defiance.

Amavasya had taken everything from him.

Madhav's sobs echoed into the desolate night, his voice hoarse from grief. "I've lost both my sons," he cried, clutching the edge of the cursed well, his bloodstained hands trembling. "And Gayatri... my beautiful wife. If only my children hadn't been born on an Amavasya night... at least one of them might have survived."

He wept uncontrollably, his anguish raw and uncontained. Nearby, Gayatri's mother stood with tears streaming down her face. In a trembling voice, she whispered, "It was true, Madhav. Everything Vetalbhadra said... it was all true. This is all because of us, beta."

Madhav, lost in his pain, kept repeating, "Both my sons are gone... both of them..."

Gathering her strength, Gayatri's mother placed a gentle hand on his shoulder. Her voice, though soft, carried the weight of a truth too heavy to bear. "Madhav, not two... three."

The words hit Madhav like a thunderclap, but in his haze of grief, they barely registered. He shook his head. "What are you saying?"

Gayatri's mother gripped his shoulder firmly, forcing him to face her. "Madhav," she said, her voice trembling, "you didn't lose two sons. Gayatri had three children."

Madhav blinked at her, his tear-filled eyes narrowing in confusion. "Three?"he repeated, shaking his head. "I don't understand. I only had two sons. Rudra and—"

She interrupted him, tears spilling down her cheeks as she fell to her knees. "No, beta. There were three. Three sons. One... before you married Gayatri."

Madhav stared at her in stunned silence, unable to process her words. "What?"he asked, his voice barely a whisper. "What are you saying? Are you telling me Gayatri... before... before me?"

Her tears came harder now, and she joined her hands in apology. "Yes, Madhav. Gayatri had a child before she married you. I beg you to forgive us. We thought... we thought, we could leave the past behind and give her a new beginning. We never meant to hurt you."Madhav's hands clenched into fists, his voice rising with rage and disbelief. "You hid something like this from me? You told me she was pure! You compared her to Ganga, to Savitri! And now... now you're telling me this?

"Gayatri's mother bowed her head, her shame evident in her every movement. "I know, beta. I know we betrayed your trust. But we did it for Gayatri. We thought the past wouldn't matter, that you would never have to know."

Madhav stepped back, his mind spinning. His grief was now intertwined with a sense of betrayal so profound it felt like a fresh wound. His voice broke as he shouted, "I deserved to know the truth! Gayatri deserved to tell me herself!"

The revelation hung heavy in the air, deepening the already suffocating silence of the cursed night.

Gayatri's mother began speaking, her voice trembling with a mixture of reverence and sorrow. "This happened years ago, Madhav. It was during the time of Baisakh Purnima when a baba visited our home. That baba... he was none other than Gaurakhi Baba."

Madhav's expression darkened, but he remained silent, listening as she continued. "There was an aura about him, Madhav. A divine glow on his face, a brilliance in his very presence. His eyes held a magnetic pull, his voice was melodious, and his entire being seemed to radiate the essence of the divine. It was as if God himself had stepped into our home."

She paused, her hands clutching the edge of her saree. "He wore wooden earrings, a black dog's figure hung from his neck, and his lips constantly murmured the name of Shiva. Gayatri, who was always drawn to spiritual matters, ran to me, her eyes sparkling with excitement. 'Maa,' she said, 'Look, a great guru has come to our home! A siddh saint!'"

Her voice wavered as she continued. "When we asked his name, he said, 'Names are for humans. I bear the name given by the Creator.' He then called himself Gaurakhi."

Madhav, his face pale and drawn, clenched his fists. "And this Gaurakhi Baba... what did he do?" he asked, his voice thick with suspicion.

Gayatri's mother sighed deeply, her eyes filled with regret. "We thought he had come to bless our family, to guide us. But what followed changed everything. Gaurakhi did not come as just a saint. He carried with him a destiny—one we could not escape."

She paused, her eyes searching Madhav's face for understanding, before continuing. "Gayatri was young, impressionable, and so full of faith in him. And that faith... led to choices we cannot undo."

Gayatri's mother's voice trembled as she continued, her words heavy with the weight of the past.

"We never thought such a thing could happen, Madhav. But what can one do when love takes hold? Love is a truth that neither cares for gain nor loss, and it blinds you to everything else. Gaurakhi Baba began visiting our home every Monday, his voice carrying a power that seemed to call to Gayatri's very soul. She would run to him at the sound of his arrival, her face lighting up as if he carried all the answers to her unspoken questions. Over time, his words began to linger in her mind, and soon, she could talk of nothing else but him."

Her eyes grew misty, the memories flooding back. "Day and night, she would think of him, speak of him, and lose herself in his presence. As parents, we started noticing the changes in her. You know how it is—mothers and fathers can sense when their child is walking a different path. Slowly, it became clear to us. Gayatri was in love with Gaurakhi Baba."

Madhav's fists tightened, his body trembling as Gayatri's mother continued. "It wasn't something we could easily accept, especially not from Gaurakhi Baba's side. But with Gayatri, there was no doubt—she was completely devoted to him. Her love for him grew stronger by the day. We tried to warn Gaurakhi Baba, to tell him that our daughter's feelings for him were not right, that he needed to leave and not come back. But he ignored us. Every Monday, without fail, he would return, and Gayatri would wait eagerly for him."

Her voice cracked with emotion. "We didn't know what to make of it. Something about all this didn't sit right with us. So, I told Gayatri's father to follow Gaurakhi Baba one day, to find out the truth. It was a Monday, and like always, Gaurakhi came. After he left, Gayatri's father followed him. What he discovered left us shaken."

She paused for a moment, her hands trembling. "He followed Gaurakhi to a hut on the outskirts of the village. There, Gaurakhi met with a man—a tantrik named Vetalbhadra. We had heard of him before; he was known for his dark rituals. Gayatri's father hid and listened to their conversation. Vetalbhadra spoke with a strange fervor, telling Gaurakhi, 'You have taken the first step. You have ensnared Gayatri, a pure-hearted woman, in your love. Her devotion to you is unwavering, exactly what we needed.'"

Her voice grew quieter, almost a whisper. "Vetalbhadra then said, 'The night of the full moon is approaching. On that night, you must confess your love to her. When she accepts your love, take her hand and embrace her. The mantra I've given you will merge your spirit with hers, and you will turn to ash. That will be your end.'"

Gayatri's mother shuddered as she recounted the moment. "Hearing this, Gayatri's father and I ran back to the village as fast as we could. We couldn't believe what we had heard. We told Gayatri everything—about Gaurakhi, about Vetalbhadra, about their plans. But she wouldn't listen, Madhav. She refused to believe a single word. To her, Gaurakhi Baba was everything—her savior, her love, her entire world."

Her voice broke as tears welled in her eyes. "She told us we were wrong, that we didn't understand him. She said she would rather die than live without him. In her heart, she had already accepted him as her husband."

Gayatri's mother hesitated before speaking, her voice trembling as she recounted the horrifying events of that night.

"We thought, perhaps, Gayatri might change with time. But Madhav, instead of turning back, she was consumed by her love for Gaurakhi Baba. And then, the night we feared the most arrived. Gayatri ran away from home. When we noticed the doors of the house open in the dead of night, we didn't make a sound. Quietly, we went out searching for her, but we didn't know where to start. The fear in our hearts was suffocating—fear for our daughter, fear for our honor. If word got out that Gayatri was infatuated with a wandering baba, the shame would have been unbearable."

Her eyes darkened as the memories took hold. "It was a new moon night, as we had dreaded. Vetalbhadra had chosen this very night to summon Gayatri, and we knew we had no time to waste. Her father and I made our way towards the outskirts of the village, our hearts pounding in terror. When we finally reached the spot, we saw what we had feared most. Gayatri was there, and so was Gaurakhi Baba."

She paused, her breath catching as the images returned vividly to her mind. "What we saw, Madhav, was beyond anything we could have imagined. Gayatri and Gaurakhi Baba were locked in an embrace, and a divine light, blinding and otherworldly, radiated from Gaurakhi. The light poured from him into Gayatri, and its brilliance was such that it seemed to outshine every lamp in the universe. Vetalbhadra stood nearby, chanting mantras with a voice that reverberated like a thousand drums. All around the village, earthen lamps were lit to ward off evil spirits, but the light emanating from Gaurakhi was unparalleled."

Madhav's expression was frozen in disbelief as Gayatri's mother continued, her voice trembling. "Slowly, Gaurakhi Baba's body began to disintegrate into ash, the radiant light within him dimming as it poured into Gayatri. Vetalbhadra's eyes were bloodshot, his face a mask of pain and determination, as if he were holding back some immense force. Finally, Gaurakhi was gone, his entire being reduced to ash, and Gayatri collapsed, unconscious. From the pile of ash where Gaurakhi once stood, a small, divine child emerged—beautiful and radiant, with a glow that could not be described."

Her voice cracked as she recalled the moment. "Vetalbhadra, his body trembling, placed his hand on the child's head and chanted more mantras. When we saw Gayatri lying motionless, we ran to her, desperate to save our daughter. We didn't understand what was happening or what this child was. We only knew that we wanted our Gayatri back."

She paused, tears streaming down her face. "But Vetalbhadra spoke to us, his voice calm despite the chaos. He said, 'It is good that you have come. I was about to bring this child to your home. Take him—he is your son now. But know this, he is no ordinary child. His body may be human, but he carries the souls of many, including Gaurakhi. He will be the vessel for future Gaurakhis, the bearer of eternal power. He is the antidote to the curse of the Lasso Kumbh and the gift of this village's redemption.'"

Gayatri's mother shook her head, her voice breaking. "We couldn't understand a word of what he was saying. All we knew was that we needed Gayatri, not this strange child. Ignoring his warnings, we left the child there and carried our unconscious daughter back home. As we fled, I heard Vetalbhadra's words—words that haunt me to this day."

Her voice dropped to a whisper. "He said, 'Mark my words. If Gayatri marries or bears children, every child born to her will come on a night like this, and they will bear the curse of the Lasso. The cycle of these wandering souls will continue, and their children will never know peace. Look at the mark on this child's back—the dharma chakra—it is a sign of his destiny.'"

Gayatri's mother shivered. "But we paid no heed to his words. We brought Gayatri home, and when she regained consciousness, she realized what had happened. She knew Gaurakhi Baba was gone, reduced to ash. The next day, the village was in uproar. They found Vetalbhadra's lifeless body, his eyes blood-red, lying where the ritual had taken place. Strangely, that night, no child had been born in the village, and no one bore the curse. People whispered that perhaps Vetalbhadra had sacrificed himself to protect the village from evil."

Her voice trailed off, and she fell silent.

Gayatri's mother, after a long pause, continued her story, her voice heavy with regret and sorrow.

"That was the day, Madhav," she began, her eyes clouded with memories, "when we decided to find a suitable match for Gayatri. That's when we found you. We hid the truth, Madhav. How could we tell anyone? Even if we had, who would have believed us? Whether it was a miracle or something else entirely, I still don't know. But that night... that child..."

Her voice faltered, and she fell silent, leaving the room steeped in tension. Madhav sat still, his face pale, struggling to process what he had just heard.

Finally, in a trembling voice, he asked, "And... what about the child? What happened to him?"

Gayatri's mother froze, her expression unreadable. "What child?" she replied, her voice laced with hesitation.

"The child," Madhav pressed, "the one born from Gaurakhi and Gayatri's union. What happened to him?"

Gayatri's mother sighed deeply, the weight of her secrets pressing down on her. "We tried, Madhav. We tried to find him. We searched everywhere, but one night..." She hesitated, her voice breaking, "that small, innocent child disappeared. Just vanished. We looked for him for days, but he was gone. Gone without a trace."

Finally, there had to be some trace of Gayatri's first child. Madhav's restlessness was palpable, and though he was not the child's father, the boy had been born to his wife, and he felt a deep, unsettling concern. He had asked repeatedly, but Gayatri's mother had no answer—no explanation of where the child had gone, or even a trace, any mark, any sign of him.

Madhav, unable to bear the uncertainty any longer, was walking away, his eyes heavy with sorrow, when suddenly, from behind him, Gayatri's mother called out. "Yes," she said, her voice soft but carrying a hint of revelation, "there was something on his back... a mark, like a wheel..."

Madhav stood abruptly, his face a mask of shock and confusion. He said nothing as he turned and walked away, leaving Gayatri's mother alone with her guilt and memories.

The narrative shifted back to the present. Gaurakhi stood silently, his body now strong and his wounds healed as if centuries of pain and decay had been erased in moments. His eyes gleamed with the knowledge of a thousand lifetimes, as if he had journeyed across endless realms and returned with the weight of their truths. He stood still, a faint smile playing on his lips, as though he had uncovered answers to questions long forgotten.

CHAPTER FOUR

The Chamera

Gaurakhi bid farewell to the house where he had been staying, spending a few more days in the village. By now, the villagers had grown familiar with him, and whispers of his presence travelled from one household to another until the entire village knew about him. Many now regarded him as a saviour, a messiah who might hold the key to breaking the curse of the **Lasso Kumbh.**

But Gaurakhi, sitting quietly on the outskirts of the village, carried a storm of questions within him. The hopes of the villagers weighed heavily on him, but he doubted his own strength. The days passed quickly, and before he knew it, the dreaded night of *amavasya* had arrived.

That evening, an eight-year-old girl, desperate and frantic, began searching for Gaurakhi. She had heard from the villagers that he might be near the infamous well—a sinister place whispered to have claimed the lives of countless women. When she arrived, her small figure illuminated by the pale moonlight, she found him seated silently by the well, his back turned to her.

"Gaurakhi Baba!" she called out, her voice trembling but determined. "Please come with me. My mother is in danger. She keeps mentioning the *Lasso* spell. You're the only one who can save her. Please, Baba, you have to help!"

Gaurakhi turned to her, his expression heavy with weariness. "Child,"** he said gently, "I can't fight that magic anymore. The world beyond this one, the one tied to that curse... it's not meant to be seen by human eyes. Each time I look into it, I feel weaker, as if I'm losing a part of myself. The answers I seek never come, only more questions. And with every question, I grow more powerless. How can I help your mother when I can't even help myself?"

The girl clasped her hands tightly, pleading with him, but Gaurakhi shook his head, his face etched with sorrow. Finally, seeing her mother in mortal peril and Gaurakhi unwilling to help, the girl's desperation turned to anger.

"You're no savior!" she cried. "You're just a coward who hides behind his words!"

Unable to face her fury, Gaurakhi turned his back to her, silently enduring her accusations. The girl, still fuming, noticed something unusual.

"Baba," she said, her tone softening slightly, "what's happening to your back? It looks like it's burning."

He sighed. "It happens every **amavasya** night," he admitted.

The girl moved closer, pointing at the intricate markings on his back, which glowed faintly red. "There's something strange about these chakra-like symbols," she said, her voice laced with curiosity. "They're glowing now, brighter than before. Maybe that's why you're feeling the burning."

Gaurakhi nodded absently. "Yes, perhaps that's the reason," he murmured, as though speaking more to himself than to her.

Despite her efforts, the girl couldn't convince Gaurakhi to move. Frustrated and defeated, she sat down beside him. Moments later, her father arrived, breathless and panicked, searching for her.

"There you are!" he exclaimed, relief flooding his voice. "What are you doing here? Don't you know this well is a graveyard on *amavasya* nights? Come home now!"

The girl looked at Gaurakhi, then back at her father. "I was talking to—" She stopped mid-sentence, glancing around. Gaurakhi had vanished, melting into the shadows as if he were never there.

Her father frowned. "Talking to whom?" he asked.

"No one," the girl replied quietly, clutching his hand as they walked away from the cursed well.

Gaurakhi was restless, unsettled by the decision he had made. Despite the girl calling out to him, he had been unable to offer her any help. He blamed himself, his thoughts spiraling with regret. After some time, exhaustion overcame him, and he finally drifted off to sleep. In the depths of his slumber, something strange occurred—he felt as though a gust of wind had entered his body, and in that moment, he sensed an unfamiliar surge of energy. He felt better, more alive than before.

The following day, news spread across India about the **Charter Act of 1813**, where the British announced their investment of one lakh rupees towards education. The intentions behind this were crystal clear: they wanted to understand India's culture in depth, so they could more easily transform it into a colony. Lord Macaulay's name was being thrown around more than ever. Around the same time, a report emerged from Mandu village—another discovery by the British. They had unearthed an ancient artifact: a Shiva temple, known locally as the Red Temple, or Madhav, or Khandar by the villagers. The British were investigating this temple, and while there was a strange sense of joy among the villagers, there was also a lingering unease.

At the same time, Macaulay's words were often repeated, **"A single shelf of a good European library is worth the whole native literature of India and Arabia."** Gaurakhi found this unsettling, especially as he thought back to the girl's cryptic words about a chakra on his back. The connection between the British discovery of the Red Temple, and what she had said, began to weigh heavily on his mind.

The thought was too much to ignore. Gaurakhi hurried to find the village artist, Shyam. He searched through the lanes, desperate to speak to him. When he finally found him, Gaurakhi wasted no time in asking, "Please, can you draw the exact chakra I have on my back? I need it to be as precise as possible."

Shyam agreed, and hours later, the artist handed him the drawing. As Gaurakhi looked at it, his heart skipped a beat. The chakra was an exact replica of the one he had seen in his dreams—the same as the one on the walls of the Red Temple in Mandu. His breath caught in his throat. The resemblance was uncanny, and a strange chill ran through him. How could this be? The symbol on his back, which he had never fully understood, now seemed to hold an undeniable connection to something much larger.

Gaurakhi's mind raced. Was it a coincidence that the British were so interested in the Red Temple, or was there a deeper connection between this ancient site and the symbol he carried? And more troubling—what did this mean for him? His entire body seemed to tremble as he stared at the drawing, a sense of foreboding rising within him. Gaurakhi now realized that the child they had been talking about was none other than himself. His eyes widened in recognition, as if a forgotten truth had suddenly been resurrected. It's me... I am Gayatri and Gaurakhi's son, he thought, a strange feeling washing over him. The very source of this magic, this mystery, was within him. Yet, as the realization dawned, Gaurakhi was left with a multitude of questions. How could this be possible?

This can't be, he thought. It's impossible for me to be Gayatri's son. The very idea defied reason. After all, this was a matter that stretched back thousands of years. How can I be alive after so many centuries? And if I am, then how is my body still so youthful, still so full of vigor, when it should have aged, withered, long ago? If I've truly lived for thousands of years, then whose youth am I bearing now?

But then, he looked again at the mark on his back, the intricate design that resembled a wheel, a symbol that had first appeared near the red temple. The sight of it made his heart race, for it seemed to confirm what he had been afraid to admit. This is me, he thought with a sense of certainty creeping over him.

The dreams of Gaurakhnath, the strange connection between his own existence and the ancient teachings, all pointed to one undeniable conclusion: I am the one they spoke of.

The questions gnawed at him relentlessly. How could I, after all these years, still be alive on this earth? It was as though his very soul was being tested, torn between the overwhelming truth of his existence and the confusion that followed it.

Gaurakhi was surrounded by many questions. But understanding the nature of the soul was crucial. Gaurakhnath Dev's words were on his mind: "Without knowing it, do not proceed with this process. It can only meet that soul once. I had to understand it; it possesses a terrifying power. It feels tainted, as if it has been greatly tormented."

Gaurakhi's mind was occupied with questions about the connection between the magic and that tainted soul. He continued to move towards the village.

It was raining, the season was monsoon. There was a lot of commotion in the village as everyone was collecting soil.

Gaurakhi asked, "Why are you all collecting soil like this, so much of it? What kind of village is this? And why?"

The response came: "Baba, you should leave. The village will be in darkness for a month, and this soil is the path to that darkness. Before the rain and Diwali, many lamps will need to be lit every day, and they will be made from this village's soil, especially from near the well."

Gaurakhi asked, "Isn't the soil from other places also soil?"

The reply was: "It is soil, but it cannot bring peace. It cannot stop it. It cannot burn and care for it with love."

Gaurakhi was puzzled, "What are you saying? This seems like a village of lunatics."

The response was: "You could say that, but it's not a village of lunatics; it's a village of cursed souls. It seems you're also from the West. A white skin does not understand the essence of the soul."

Gaurakhi was completely confused. He drank his chilam and went to sleep, wondering how to proceed. He had no clarity.As night passed, the dawn might reveal some secrets. Gaurakhnath, carrying his alms bowl, went into the village. Everyone respected him, knowing the miracles within Gaurakhi.

But in every house he visited, there were sacks of soil. Conversations were happening:

In some places, there was a lot of commotion, while in others, calmness – "The quota for this time is completed," and in some houses, "Thank God, we got the soil this time."

Gaurakhi couldn't understand what was going on. He was taken in by a family where he had gone to ask for alms. The woman of the house said, "Baba, please come inside and sanctify our home. I will bring food for you shortly."

Gaurakhi said, "Thank you. Can I ask you something?"

"Yes, of course, Maharaj."

Gaurakhi asked, "Why is there such commotion everywhere for soil?"

The woman replied, "Baba, this is preparation for Chamera."

Gaurakhi asked, "Chamera, what is that?"

The woman said, "Baba, we don't know what it is either, but we are afraid. We don't want any child born in our house to be possessed by that spirit, the one with black magic."

"You know well, and the villagers have great hope that you will deliver us from this."

Gaurakhi thanked her and asked, "What is to be done about Chamera?"

The woman explained that everyone in the village waits for the first rain. As soon as it rains, they need to bring the soil home and keep it safely in their yard or somewhere else.

Gaurakhi then said, "I have heard that from many houses. From what I've gathered, this soil is used to make lamps, and these lamps are lit during the Amavasya that falls between the rain and Diwali."

The woman confirmed, "You are right. This helps us keep away the dangers and the shadow of the dark spirit. But it is essential to remember one thing: The soil must be from near the well, and it must be kept at home. Lamps must be kept burning around it to attract many winged ants. These ants are drawn to the light and then drop their wings into the soil."

"When the number of wings is correct, mix those wings into the soil while chanting the mantra. This task is reserved only for men, specifically those who are over 50 years old. Gaurakhi asks what the mantra is. The mantra is not revealed to us, nor do we women know it. You will find the mantra among the men of the village who are over 50 years old.

Alright, tell me more.

The woman asks if Gaurakhi needs anything else—water or a couple of rotis.

Gaurakhi replies, "No, I just need to know the story; please continue."

The woman explains that the soil needs to be used to make lamps in the afternoon when the sun is overhead. This must be done on that day. Also, the lamps should not be lit with oil but with ghee during the time of Sahrad.

Gaurakhi inquires why this is done with ghee.

We do not know, and no one in the village knows. This is called the 'Chamera's Curse.'

The 'Chamera's Curse' is approaching, and everyone has started preparing.

Gaurakhi leaves with a lot on his mind and the villagers' hopes weighing on him. He felt that he had been given a hint, and it seemed that this curse might be related to the story. But how to start, from where to begin—he couldn't figure it out. Gaurakhi begins to smoke his chilam and thinks,

"I need to do something, but how should I start? The story of Chamera might lead me to this curse. But how should I begin?"

After a while of thinking and pondering deeply, Gaurakhi decides,

"It seems I need to first meet an old man to learn this mantra. Perhaps this mantra will help and clarify some of the confusion."

Gaurakhi approaches an elderly man and asks about the mantra. The old man tells him that he cannot reveal the mantra as it could be used to make lamps, but he can write it down for him. The old man writes the mantra on a stick and some wet clay.

"Chamera Shantam Bhutva, Tvam visheshyasangamaya...

Chamera, Vayam Gramavasi Kshamamyachchhama, Raja Varmanasya Doshanam...

Chamera, Esh Gramah Tava Asti, Iha Pashya Tasmin Diye vishvarasa Asti."

(Meaning: "Chamera, be calm and meet Vishva. Chamera, we, the villagers, ask for forgiveness for the mistakes of King Varman Chakra. Chamera, this village is yours, and here you can see that the lamp contains Vishva.")

Gaurakhi needs to understand this mantra. Who exactly is Chamera? He needs to resolve the puzzle involving Chamera, King Varman, and Vishesh.

Gaurakhi asks about Chamera, but the old man says, "Do not mention Chamera's name. I now understand more about it."

Gaurakhi inquires with many people, but everyone refuses to talk about it or claims not to know anything.

Meanwhile, the terror of the British in the village is escalating. They are discussing among themselves that it is difficult to make these Indians work as slaves because their religion is keeping them strong. As long as they are not separated from their religion, they cannot be enslaved. They need to involve the village chief, Dharampal. Another British officer says, "Dharampal? No, he's an old man who knows everything. Even though he's 85 years old, he knows this village better than anyone. That's why everyone trusts him, and his decisions are considered very authoritative." Gaurakhi listens carefully to their conversation and then sets out in search of Dharampal. Upon finding out from the villagers, Gaurakhi learns about Dharampal:

Dharampal was one who did not believe in Chamera, but his wife fully believed in Chamera. During the Shradh period, Dharampal did not collect soil in the first rain nor make lamps. The curse worsened to the point where a boy was born to his son, and shortly after, his daughter began to be possessed. As the possession intensified, talk of magic began, leading Dharampal to flee. Sweating profusely, he didn't know where to go. He ran to the Kamakhya temple. Before he could perform any remedy there, his daughter-in-law had already sacrificed her child. Seeing this, Dharampal broke down and spent 30 years trying to understand the curse.

Gaurakhi meets Dharampal. Upon seeing Gaurakhi, Dharampal says, "Baba, I have heard a lot about you, and I knew you would come here one day." "As you know," he began, his voice carrying a weight of experience, "you've come here to learn about the **Chamera**." He paused, letting the silence settle before continuing. "I have felt the truth of this matter very closely, more intimately than most. And as the village head, I have repeatedly made this known to the British authorities. But to them, it is nothing more than a story—a tale, a lie, something concocted from my own imagination." He coughed weakly, his frail body betraying his age. "I am sick now, perhaps with only a few years left, if I'm lucky. I may not have much time left to see this through."

His eyes glimmered with a mixture of resignation and unyielding determination. "But you must know this—there is more truth to this than they realize. The **Chamera** is not just a myth. It is real. And I have felt its presence, its weight, on my own life."

To know Chamera's story, you will need to hold on tightly. This story is not of a day or two. When I lost my family and reached Kamakhya, I had to travel from Nalanda to Taxila to know the truth. Yes, this secret must be known from Taxila.

Gaurakhi was stunned. His eyes widened in disbelief as he repeated, "Taxila? Is it really connected to Taxila?" He shook his head, as though trying to shake off the weight of what he was hearing. "I can't believe it. To think this story stretches all the way back to Taxila—it's hard to fathom."

The more he tried to comprehend, the more impossible it seemed. The **Lasso Kumbh**—the entire idea—was beyond his grasp. The complexity of it all, the way it interwove with ancient history, felt like a knot he couldn't untangle.

Turning to Dharampal, his voice filled with urgency, Gaurakhi said, "Please, tell me everything. I will believe whatever you say. Every word."

And with that, Gaurakhi fell into a quiet attentiveness, his mind bracing itself for the story that Dharampal was about to share. As Dharampal began, Gaurakhi was pulled into the narrative, each word, each detail, deepening the mystery and drawing him further into the intricate web of truths and secrets that had been hidden for so long. Dharampal, with a steady voice, began to unfold the story, layer by layer, revealing every intricate detail as though each word was carefully chosen. He spoke with such conviction, as if the tale had been etched into his very soul. As he narrated, he placed his own story before Gaurakhi, like an offering of truth that had long been waiting to be shared.

Every word was measured, every pause deliberate, as Dharampal weaved the tale, offering not just the facts, but the wisdom he had gathered over years of understanding. Gaurakhi listened intently, his mind absorbing each detail, feeling the weight of the story grow heavier with every passing moment.

One day in Taxila, I found a book. An ancient story from many years ago, a story similar to what we know from the Vedas, was in that book.

This story is set in a time long forgotten, lost in the ancient world of myths and magic. I found an old book one day in the ancient city of Taxila. Its pages were brittle, the ink fading with age, but within its words lay a tale that seemed to belong to the Vedic era, intertwined with the mystical verses of the Yajur Veda. As I delved deeper into the study of the Vedas, I encountered references to dark magic and something called **Chamera** — a word that sent a shiver down my spine.

According to the texts, a **Chamera** was a being neither fully human nor entirely animal, something born under the veil of darkness, during the night of the new moon. Such creatures were rare, born from the shadowy fringes of the world, embodying both the human and the beast within. Feared and revered, their existence was an enigma, a hidden secret of the universe.

CHAPTER FIVE

Aashun

But this story is not merely about ancient scripts; it is about an event that took place many centuries ago. A time when two great masters of dark arts, Vaayun and his nephew Vishva, lived in the mystic land of **Mayan civilization.** These two were known far and wide for their mastery over woodcraft, though their talents went far beyond the physical realm. They were believed to hold powers that could alter reality itself, creating life from inanimate objects.

Their fame reached the ears of **Raja Varman Chakra** , the righteous ruler of the village of Munda. Raja Varman Chakra was not an ordinary king. His reputation stretched far beyond his lands, known for his sense of justice, wisdom, and compassion. So revered was he that his subjects often referred to him as an incarnation of Lord Ram. His decisions were always fair, his heart pure, and he ruled his people with a deep sense of duty and responsibility.

When Raja Varman heard of Vaayun and Vishva's incredible talents, he was both intrigued and skeptical. Could it really be true? Could these two artisans indeed possess such profound mastery of their craft that they could breathe life into lifeless wood?

"I have heard much about Vaayun and Vishva," Raja Varman said one evening to his courtiers, his voice calm but curious. "But can they truly craft anything from wood? Can their skill really bring something to life? I find it hard to believe. Bring them to my court. I must see with my own eyes whether art can truly give birth to life."

Upon the king's command, a troop of soldiers was dispatched to fetch Vaayun and Vishva from their village. The journey took them to a place where a great crowd had gathered, watching in awe as the young Vishva displayed his artistry. Even from afar, the soldiers could see that Vishva was no ordinary craftsman. He worked with wood as though it was a living extension of himself. He had carved birds, insects, and creatures so lifelike that they almost seemed ready to take flight or crawl off the table.

As the soldiers approached, they realized that the stories they had heard were indeed true. This young artist possessed a gift unlike any other. His hands moved with precision, breathing life into the wood. And the crowd that had gathered around him was a testament to the power of his craft.

The soldiers told Vaayun and Vishva that they had been summoned by the great Raja Varman himself. Hearing this, both master and apprentice were overjoyed. This was the moment they had been waiting for—a chance to showcase their art in front of a king renowned for his wisdom and fairness. With great anticipation, they dressed themselves in their finest robes and prepared to leave for the royal court.

On their journey, Vaayun, ever the mentor, spoke to Vishva, offering him advice for the meeting with the king. "Remember, Vishva," he said, his voice low but firm, "when you stand before the king, speak little. Let your art speak for you. Do not allow any doubt to enter your mind. This is not just a test of my skills, but yours as well. Today, we will not only show our craft but prove that our mastery can withstand the scrutiny of the greatest ruler."

Though Vaayun was Vishva's mentor, there was something about the younger artist that often left even the master in awe. Vishva's mind was filled with innovation, and his vision extended beyond what was traditionally taught. He was an idealist, always striving for something new, something greater. While Vaayun represented the depth of ancient knowledge and skill, Vishva's thinking often soared into the realms of modernity and creativity. Together, they were a perfect balance—the wisdom of the past meeting the potential of the future.

The road to the royal court was long, but their excitement grew with every step. Vishva, though young, carried the weight of not only his uncle's teachings but also his own untested ideas. His hands, though still, seemed to pulse with the energy of untapped potential, waiting to be unleashed in front of the king.

As they approached the towering gates of the palace, the grandeur of the place didn't intimidate them. Rather, it inspired them. For Vaayun, it was a chance to honor the ancient art he had spent his life mastering. For Vishva, it was an opportunity to show that art was not just a craft, but a form of creation that could transcend the physical world and touch the divine.

King Varman sat on his throne, his voice calm yet commanding. "I have but one question for you," he said, his eyes locking on the artisan, Vayun. "This question will test both your skill and your wisdom."

Vayun stood, his heart racing. He had never seen the King so serious before.

"Create something for me," the King continued, "something that has never seen itself, and when it did, the world never saw it again."

Vayun's mind spun. What could it be? His hands trembled, sweat beading on his brow as if the golden opportunity slipping from his grasp. Just then, a small voice cut through his thoughts.

"Baba, it's easy," said Vishva, Vayun's son, tugging at his father's robe. "Just make a man looking at his reflection in a pond. I'll make a small flower next to him."

Vayun stared at his son in disbelief. Of course! He set to work, his hands moving swiftly, carving a figure of a man gazing into a pond. Vishva began crafting a delicate flower at the man's feet.

As the King watched, he slowly rose to his feet and clapped, the sound reverberating through the grand hall. "Brilliant! You have recognized it—Narcissus! The man whose beauty even he did not comprehend, yet when he saw it, the world lost him." The King continued, his voice filled with admiration. "Narcissus, so beautiful that even nature itself was in awe. The forest nymphs, gods, and even the flowers adored him. Yet, despite all the admiration, he remained ignorant of his own splendor. It was his tragic flaw."

Queen Mayra, who had been sitting beside the King, joined in. Her voice soft yet filled with an otherworldly resonance. "Indeed, his beauty was his curse. He shunned love, even rejecting a forest nymph who offered him her heart. Spurned, the nymph cursed him: 'One day, you will see what you have denied, and on that day, your beauty will destroy you.'" The Queen's eyes gleamed as she continued the tale, her voice mesmerizing the entire court. "And so it came to pass. One day, Narcissus wandered deep into the forest, unaware of the curse upon him. Rain had filled a small pond, its surface like a mirror. He leaned in, curious, and for the first time, he saw himself."

"He was frozen, entranced by his own reflection, unable to look away, lost in his beauty. And so, he remained, staring, until he became one with the earth itself. From his remains bloomed a flower, which we now know as the Narcissus." As Queen Mayra finished her story, Vayun placed the final touches on his carving, depicting the beautiful youth staring into the water. On the other side of the table, little Vishva presented his small but perfect flower. The King was overjoyed, clapping enthusiastically. "Magnificent! Both of you have captured the essence of the story! Vayun, your craftsmanship, and Vishva, your keen insight." He motioned to a servant. "Gold will be your reward, but more than that, from this day forward, you will both remain in my court, creating works of art to adorn this palace. Your talents shall be used to beautify my kingdom."

Vayun and Vishva beamed with pride. The King's court had always been known for its grandeur, but now, their creations would grace its walls and halls. King Varman, a devout follower of Lord Shiva, had always believed in the blessings of the gods. His generosity and love for his people had earned him their undying loyalty. His reputation as a wise and just ruler was unmatched. Yet, behind the grandeur of his rule, there was always one person whose counsel he valued above all others—Rishi Ramanuj, the great sage.

Rishi Ramanuj, who had dedicated his life to the pursuit of Brahmatva, advised the King on all matters of state and spirituality. The bond between them was strong, and not a single decision was made without consulting the wise sage.

But not everything in King Varman's court was as it seemed. Behind the regal facade of Queen Mayra lay a secret that no one knew. Rani Mayra, the name given to her by King Varman, was born Chandavati. She was a woman of exceptional beauty, and from the moment King Varman laid eyes on her, he was smitten. Chandavati's charm and grace were nothing short of enchanting, and her radiant beauty captured the king's heart entirely. In the way that love often works, King Varman found himself desperate to know everything about her—her likes, her dislikes, every small detail that would bring him closer to her soul.

He soon discovered that the queen had a deep fondness for Greek mythology. She lived within the stories of ancient Greece. The tales of **Odyssey**, the **Trojan War** , **Prometheus**, **Narcissus**, **Erysichthon**, and **Cupid and Psyche** captivated her heart, but it was the tragic and powerful stories like that of **Icarus** and **Prometheus** that truly fascinated her. These myths filled her world with meaning, and the king, eager to win her affection, began to weave them into their conversations.

Slowly, with every mention of these stories, the queen, Chandavati, began to gravitate toward the king. Love blossomed between them, and as their relationship deepened, King Varman, with a tender smile, one day said to her, "Chandavati, this name does not suit you. Just as your nose reflects your tastes, your name should reflect your spirit. From now on, not just I, but our entire court will call you by a new name—Mayra."

The queen, touched by his words and the thought behind them, found the name beautiful. It resonated with her. After their marriage, she embraced her new name fully. She began spending more and more of her time delving into books of ancient tales, especially those of

Greek mythology. She kept herself immersed in those stories, as they held her heart and mind, and she became a keeper of knowledge from those ancient worlds. King Varman, a man of honor, valued his dignity above all else. If even a whisper of scandal touched his name, he would not hesitate to punish the offender, no matter who it was. The Queen knew this, and yet, her lust drove her to dangerous places, places that no one in the court could ever know about.

One afternoon, as Vayun was working on a new creation—a small, lifelike animal made of wood—Queen Mayra approached him. "Does it move?" she asked, her voice teasing as she examined the tiny wooden creature. "If I push it with my finger, will it walk? Or will the wind carry it forward?"

Vayun chuckled, wiping the sweat from his brow. "Maharani, it can move in any way you wish, but it will never have life. Its limbs will bend, and it will appear to walk, but it will always remain a lifeless thing."The Queen's eyes gleamed with mischief. "Can you make a bull? A small one, the size of my finger? And will it move if I push it?"

Vayun laughed again. "A bull, Maharani? Yes, I can make it. And it will move just as you wish—everything but life itself can be given to it."

The Queen leaned closer, her voice low. "Everything?" she whispered. "Are you sure? Can you make one as large as a real bull? Big enough for a man to ride?"

Vayun was taken aback, confused by her question. "Maharani, I do not understand. A wooden bull the size of a real one?" The Queen's smile deepened, her eyes locking onto his. "Yes, a bull. Large, strong, and capable of everything a real one can do. Except for one thing—no life. Could you make that for me?"

Vayun hesitated, his heart pounding as he tried to make sense of the Queen's request. "Your Majesty... a bull, so large that a man could fit inside it... and you want it to move, to have everything but life? I don't understand—what would you use it for?"

Queen Mayra's lips curled into a sly smile. "That is none of your concern. All I need to know is—can you make it or not? Can you and your nephew, Vishva, create this for me? I will reward you handsomely, with jewels and riches beyond your wildest dreams. Opportunities like this don't come twice, Vayun."

Vayun shifted uncomfortably. He had always been a man of integrity, driven by the love of his craft and a desire to create beauty in the world. But the allure of wealth and the chance to expand his skills tempted him, especially since money had always been tight. He glanced at Vishva, who was watching him intently.

"Uncle, we should take the offer," Vishva said quietly, his voice urgent. "Think about it—this could set us up for life! We wouldn't have to worry about money anymore. And as for what the Queen wants to do with it, that's not our concern. We're artisans; we create, nothing more."

Vayun's conscience tugged at him, but the prospect of never having to struggle for money again, of securing a future for both of them, made him waver. Finally, he nodded, his resolve weakening under Vishva's words. "Very well, Your Majesty. We will make it. But in return, you must give us not only gold but also a house here in Mandu, where we can store our riches and live without worry."

The Queen's eyes gleamed with triumph. "It's a deal, Vayun. From tonight onward, you will begin work. There's an old, abandoned hut near the well on the outskirts of the village. I'll have it cleaned and made ready for you to live in, and behind it is a forest full of strong trees—mangroves and poplar, perfect for your project. You will work there, in secret, and only at night. During the day, you will remain at the palace, so the King does not suspect anything."

Vishva grinned, eager to begin. "We will call it 'Aashun,' not a bull, but a creation, our masterpiece."

The Queen nodded approvingly. "Yes... 'Aashun.' Now get to work. I will see to it that everything you need is provided."

As they left the palace, the winds howled outside, and an eerie stillness hung in the air. Neither Vayun nor Vishva could have known that this Aashun, this monstrous creation, would become the downfall of Mandu, a curse rather than a masterpiece.

Months passed as Vayun and Vishva toiled away in secret. Under the cover of darkness, they worked tirelessly, shaping the enormous wooden beast in the hidden grove behind the Queen's secluded hut. Rani Mayra had employed dozens of workers to ensure the materials were gathered and transported discreetly, away from the King's watchful eyes. The Aashun began to take shape—an imposing wooden bull, large enough for a man to fit inside, its intricately carved joints designed to mimic the movements of a real beast. But there was no life, only the mechanical precision of the artisans' craft.

As time went on, rumors spread throughout the village. Vayun and Vishva had become famous for their skills, and though no one knew what they were working on, everyone spoke of their extraordinary talents.

They say that "time is both a blessing and a curse," and soon enough, the day arrived when Aashun was complete. It stood in the clearing, a marvel of craftsmanship, its massive form gleaming in the moonlight. Queen Mayra arrived, her eyes wide with excitement and lustful anticipation.

When she saw the Aashun, her breath caught in her throat. It was perfect, more magnificent than she could have ever imagined. She circled the creation, unable to speak for several moments, lost in the allure of its grand design. After what seemed like an eternity, she spoke, her voice trembling with anticipation. "Is this where one enters?" she asked, pointing to the opening at the base of the beast. "Will a man fit inside?"

She turned to one of her guards, a tall, burly man named Bariam. "Get in," she ordered.

Bariam hesitated for a moment, but the Queen's command was absolute. He climbed into the wooden bull, lying down inside as instructed. The Queen watched intently, her breath quickening as she observed how perfectly his body fit within the contraption, how the design allowed his form to meld with the wooden beast. "Does it work?" she murmured, her eyes narrowing as she focused on the point where Bariam's body aligned with the wooden structure. Slowly, she saw the shift, the connection, the blending of man and machine.

Her heart raced, the hunger inside her growing uncontrollable. "It's perfect," she whispered, her voice thick with desire. She turned to Vayun and Vishva, who stood silently, awaiting her judgment. "You have done well," she said, her voice rich with satisfaction. "You will be rewarded as promised." Queen Mayra gazed at Vayu and Vishva, her eyes soft with admiration. She leaned forward, gently kissing their foreheads, then took their hands in hers. "You've done what I've longed to do for so long," she said, her voice filled with awe. "The stories I once thought were only myths, you've brought them to life. You've created the tale of Icarus. You are my Greek heroes."

Her words echoed through the room, wrapping the two men in warmth and pride. But behind her praise, there was something deeper—something that neither Vayu nor Vishva could yet understand. Queen Mayra, more than just a ruler, was also deeply immersed in the ancient magic of the Mayan civilization and the darker arts of sorcery. She often disappeared into these realms, lost in rituals and powers that many could not fathom. Vayu and Vishva, overjoyed by her words, beamed with happiness, their hearts soaring. They had never felt such joy, but there was one thing they didn't know—something they were blind to: Queen Mayra had a plan, a purpose, and they were key players in it.

As Mayra observed them, something inside her shifted. She turned to them with a sudden seriousness in her eyes, a thought lingering in her mind. "Do you know why my name was Chandavati?" she asked, her voice softer now, reflective. "My parents named me after the moon—after its beauty. They saw the moon from afar and thought it perfect. But they forgot that the moon, as beautiful as it is, has its flaws. From a distance, the moon shines so brightly, but those who have come close know its depths, its imperfections."

She smiled, a quiet, knowing smile. "Yes, I am that moon. But King Varman gave me a new name—Mayra. A name by which I am known throughout the palace. This name carries his love for me, a love that stays alive in my heart every time I hear it. Whenever someone calls me by this name, I am reminded of the moment when he gave it to me."

There was a pause, and her gaze turned tender, almost playful. "Today, I feel the same way about you both. From now on, I give you names. Vayu, you are **'Prome'**, and Vishva, you are **'Theus'**."

The two men, overwhelmed by the honor, smiled widely. Their joy was impossible to contain as they bowed to her, thanking her for the new names, for the love they felt in her words.

But deep inside, Queen Mayra couldn't help but smile to herself. Yes, these two are truly my Prometheus and Theus, she thought. They are my own creation.

And with that thought, she couldn't hold back any longer. A loud, carefree laugh erupted from her, echoing in the room, as though the universe itself was in on the secret. The sound of her laughter was full of joy, but also of something deeper—an understanding that she, like the Greek heroes she adored, had woven her own fate, and now, she was ready to see it unfold.

True to her word, the Queen filled their hands with gold and silver, riches beyond anything they had ever imagined. She had the Aashun hidden in a secret chamber deep within the palace, far from the prying eyes of the court. And there, she indulged her darkest desires.

Each night, a new man was sent into the Aashun. The Queen would lie with the beast, merging with it in her twisted fantasies, while the men inside played their roles. To the outside world, it was as if Queen Mayra had vanished into a world of her own. Only Vayun, Vishva, and a select few knew of the monstrous secret hidden in the palace.

Over time, the Queen's obsession with the Aashun grew, consuming her entirely. She cared for nothing else, not even her duties as a queen. Her lust drove her deeper into madness, as she sought pleasure not from men, but from the creation itself.

The village of Mandu, once peaceful and thriving, began to suffer. Crops failed, the animals grew restless, and the people whispered of a curse that had befallen them. Little did they know that the Aashun, this unnatural creation, had become a symbol of their impending doom.

As the final piece of their masterpiece was complete, Vayun and Vishva stood back, knowing they had not just created something extraordinary, but something dark and dangerous. The Queen's twisted desires had been brought to life in wood and metal, and now, there was no turning back.

The Aashun had been born, and with it, the fate of Mandu was sealed.

As time went on, the Queen's secret life grew darker, more dangerous. No one in the palace knew of her twisted desires except for Vayun and Vishva, who had crafted the Aashun and had become her accomplices. To protect her secret, the Queen ensured that every man who entered the Aashun either met his end or was paid off with enough gold and silver to buy his silence forever.

Countless men vanished, yet no one dared ask questions, for the Queen's will was absolute.

But then came the day when everything changed.

One night, after many secret liaisons with the Aashun, Queen Mayra suddenly fell ill. Her handmaidens surrounded her, and soon, word of her condition reached King Varaman. Physicians were summoned, and after a series of examinations, the truth came to light—Queen Mayra was pregnant.

The entire palace erupted in joy at the news. The King, who had long desired an heir, was overjoyed, believing that his time had finally come. But even during her pregnancy, the Queen continued her visits to the Aashun in secret, her obsession undiminished.

Then, on a fateful night—an ominous new moon—Queen Mayra went into labor. The palace was filled with anticipation, priests and sages whispering that the child born under such an astrological sign would be wise and powerful, destined for greatness.

But when the midwife emerged from the Queen's chambers, her face was ashen, her hands trembling.

"Maharaj..." she began, but the words caught in her throat.

King Varaman, eager for news of his child, urged her to speak. "Tell me—did the Queen give birth to a son or a daughter?" The midwife stood frozen, unable to answer. Before she could utter another word, a voice rang out from the back of the room, chilling everyone to the bone.

"A monster has been born," someone shouted. "A Chamera!"

The King staggered, unable to comprehend the words. "A Chamera?" he echoed, his voice shaking.

The midwife finally spoke, her voice barely a whisper. "The child... his body... it is not human. He has the shape of the Aashun, and his face... his face is like a man, but with horns atop his head..."

Panic spread like wildfire through the palace. The King ordered his priests and scholars to investigate. Rumors of dark magic and curses flew from one corner of the court to another. Vayun and Vishva, who had witnessed the Queen's secret over the months, realized that this was the result of the unnatural bond between the Queen and the Aashun. "It's a curse," Vishva whispered to Vayun. "This is the price for the Queen's sins, for her union with the Aashun."

Desperate to rid the palace of this abomination, the King ordered his soldiers to search for the Aashun, convinced that the source of this curse lay hidden somewhere in the kingdom. The soldiers were instructed to find the Aashun, destroy it, and kill the Chamera. The King also commanded the priests to perform rituals to cleanse the land of this dark magic.

Fear gripped Vayun and Vishva. If the soldiers found the Aashun, the truth would come to light, and they would be executed for their part in the creation. Without wasting any time, they fled into the forest and destroyed the Aashun. They burned the wood, turning it to ashes, hoping to erase all evidence of its existence.

But before they could disappear, Queen Mayra sent for them.

"You must save the Chamera," she commanded, her eyes wild with desperation. "I want him to live. Hide him where no one will find him. Do this for me, and you will be rewarded."

Knowing they had no choice, Vayun and Vishva agreed. They hid the Chamera in the same secret chamber where the Aashun had once stood. When the King's soldiers came searching, they found only ashes. The Queen lied, telling the King that the Chamera had been burned, his remains now nothing but dust and cinders.

In truth, the Chamera was very much alive.

He was no ordinary child. His body grew at an unnatural speed, and within just two months, he had the size and strength of an eight-year-old boy. His horns, like those of the Aashun, curled from his head, and his mind was terrifyingly sharp. It was as if he could think a thousand thoughts at once, processing information faster than any human could. His intelligence was beyond anything they had ever seen.

Despite his monstrous appearance, Vayun and Vishva became fond of the Chamera, raising him in secret alongside the Queen. Over time, the boy grew closer to them than he ever did to his own mother. He saw them as his true family, the only people who truly cared for him.

But as the years passed, the fear in Vayun and Vishva's hearts never left. They knew that if the Chamera was ever discovered, it would mean death—not just for him, but for all of them.

And so, the monstrous secret of the Aashun and the Chamera remained hidden, buried deep within the shadows of the palace, where only darkness and fear resided.

CHAPTER SIX

The Great Escape

Because Chamera wasn't like other humans, he slipped away from the palace and began worshiping Shiva. He hoped that his incomplete birth might find fulfillment through devotion. To conceal himself, he adopted the appearance of a monk, or Gaurakhi, covering his face with ash and coils, hiding his identity. In his devotion, he uncovered mantras powerful enough to summon or communicate with spirits. His sharp mind led him deep into the study of the Vedas and the Upanishads, and he discovered secrets that he shared only with his friends Vaayun and Vishva. His knowledge grew, and he stored his sacred texts within his secluded house in Mandu.

Chamera was elated; he had discovered something miraculous. It was something no one had ever achieved, a magic so potent it could bend the very fabric of life and death itself. Tears of joy welled in his eyes as he pondered who he could share this newfound power with.

Above all, Chamera cherished one person more than anything, even more than his mother—his brother Vishva. Vishva was Chamera's entire world. Determined, Chamera set out to find him, calling out, "Vishva! Where are you, Vishva?"

As he wandered, he overheard the murmurs of a gathering crowd in the village. Concealing himself, Chamera listened intently to the hushed, anxious voices.

"The king has killed Queen Mayra," someone said gravely. "It's all because of something to do with Aashun. And now he's captured Vishva and Vaayun. Word has it the king found out they were involved in creating Aashun, and the queen was somehow entangled in it."

Chamera's heart sank as tears streamed down his face. The pain of losing his mother was immense, but the fear of losing Vishva, his dearest companion and lifeblood, was unbearable. At the royal court, accusations flew as the crowd clamored for justice. "Vishva and vaayun misused their skills and crossed the limits of royal edicts. They should be put to death!" someone shrieked with venom. Chamera felt his heart shatter as he heard the guards mock him, calling him the spawn of the queen's 'reckless deeds.'

The king had already executed Queen Mayra in the center of the court. Now, he turned toward Vishva and vaayun with lethal intent. But just as he was about to deliver his verdict, the villagers' voices rose in a wave of desperate support. "They have done so much good! Spare their lives!"

Moved, albeit reluctantly, the king altered his decision and sentenced them to life imprisonment instead. Their prison was an ancient, towering chimney—a desolate, stone cylinder open only to the sky. The only things that fell from above were feathers from passing birds. Each night, they were given a single candle for light.

Vishva and Vaayun grew despondent. Their spirit broke under the weight of confinement, while outside, Chamera moved like a shadow, unable to reconcile his own helplessness. Each night, he plotted a way to rescue them, but the chimney was the tallest structure in both the village and the royal palace. Years passed in silence. Chamera, who had once grown rapidly, reached a halt in his growth and became fixed at his youthful size. Yet, his mind remained sharp, able to churn out thousands of thoughts in a moment, each converging on a single hope—that he might someday free Vishva and vaayun.

Inside the chimney, Vishva and Vaayun's resilience found a spark of ingenuity. Every day, Vishva collected fallen feathers and melted candle wax. Slowly, using materials from within their prison, they crafted wings—large enough to carry a human. They used wooden scraps to fashion the structure and affixed the wax-laden feathers to them.

Finally, the day of reckoning came. Their plan was to climb the rough, inner walls of the chimney and, from the top, leap into freedom. As they prepared, hope coursed through their veins. Clinging to the wall's crevices, they inched upward until they reached the summit. The sky stretched out before them, blue and endless.

vaayun inspected their makeshift wings one last time, a solemn smile on his face. He turned to Vishva. "Listen, my son. When we take flight, control is everything. Just beyond is the great sea, and above us, the blazing sun. Remember, do not fly too high or too low."

Vishva nodded confidently, "Don't worry, Father. I'll follow your words."

With a deep breath, they leaped. vaayun soared ahead, his wings holding steady. Vishva followed, exhilaration rising within him like an untamed flame. But soon, pride got the better of him. He began to ascend higher and higher, while Vaayun's calls echoed in the wind, "Vishva, stay down! Do not go too close to the sun. Listen to me!"

But Vishva was entranced, drawn by the sun's golden brilliance. The wax began to melt, and before he could react, the wings disintegrated. In an instant, Vishva plunged downward, crashing into the sea below.

vaayun watched in horror as Vishva's wings melted and he plummeted into the sea. Helpless, vaayun descended to the ground, consumed by grief. He had lost his son, his pride, and his world. The shock was too great for him to bear, and madness took hold. Days passed as vaayun hid deep within the jungle, his mind fractured.

Chamera, who had also taken refuge in the jungle, stumbled upon vaayun in his delirium. Fear gripped Chamera; he thought he had been caught. But when he recognized Vaayun, his eyes filled with tears. He rushed to him, offering water and cleaning his wounds. Chamera searched vaayun's eyes desperately for a sign of Vishva and asked repeatedly where his brother was. Vaayun, unable to form coherent words due to his madness, could only gesture incoherently, leaving Chamera with an empty ache and a gnawing fear.

It became clear to Chamera that Vishva was either in grave danger or lost. Days turned into weeks, each one feeding Chamera's growing anxiety. Finally, vaayun's mind began to clear, and he recounted the tragic tale to Chamera. After that, Chamera disappeared for days, overwhelmed by the weight of this newfound responsibility. He realized that even if Vishva was gone, he had to take care of Vaayun.

Chamera began to search for vaayun, for in the dense, shadowed forest, no one could hide as well as he could. For years, Chamera survived in the wild, praying to Shiva and finding himself. He came to understand that while he may have been physically deformed, mentally he was as powerful as a thousand men combined. His mind was capable of weaving through a labyrinth of thoughts and finding the path forward. The heart of Chamera had already shattered long ago, and with it, the hope of ever truly living again had also faded. Yet, he was neither human nor anything ordinary—he was a being caught between worlds, trying to hold himself together before he inevitably fell apart from within. Again and again, he gathered whatever strength he could muster to keep himself intact, but inside, he had already broken.

Then, one day, a sudden realization hit him. Deep inside, a feeling stirred—'I must take care of the world, just as my father did'. After the death of his mother, Mayra, Vishva had given him the love of a father, raised him, and taken care of him. Now, it was his turn. It was his responsibility to be the pillar, the support for Vishva, who had always been there for him.

"I must be the one to hold him up now," Chamera thought, as the weight of this duty settled within him, pulling him from his sorrow. The time had come for him to be the support, to give back the love and care that Vishva had so selflessly given to him.

Then, one day, they both vanished for a year. No one knew where they were or what had become of them.

Out of the blue, word reached the king's court that someone wished to present a miracle. The king paid little attention at first, engrossed in his royal duties. But when the message came that this miracle-worker claimed to have discovered the secret to bringing the dead back to life, and that the method was known as **Lasso Kumbh**, the king felt the ground shift beneath him. The name sent a chill through his spine and brought tears to his eyes. Memories of Sattu flooded his mind.

Sobbing, the king muttered, "Sattu, where are you, my son? Come back to me."

Sattu, the king's beloved son, had been born on a moonless night, under circumstances that history would never forget. In this land, it was believed that whether king or commoner, all were subject to the whims of fate and spirits.

The king's fear had always been that Sattu would be ensnared by dark forces. He spared no effort, consulting priests and sages, performing countless rituals and grand sacrifices to shield his family from this curse. The priests reassured him: "Maharaj, have no fear. We have stripped this child of all curses. No shadow of a spirit will ever darken his path."

The king, torn between relief and doubt, watched as the days turned to months and years. Eight years passed, and Sattu grew strong and bright. But then, on the eve of another moonless night, Queen Kamvati's health took a sudden turn. Healers were summoned from across the kingdom, yet none could identify her ailment. As the next dark moon approached, Kamvati began to whisper one word over and over — **Lasso**.

The king's blood ran cold as realization dawned. He felt numb, paralyzed with fear. He understood now: **Lasso Kumbh** meant the sacrifice of his son, Sattu. He knew he could not save him. The king's spirit broke, his mind unraveling with despair.

Kamvati's condition deteriorated further, and the palace was gripped with terror. If the **Lasso Kumbh** was not performed, Kamvati would either beat herself to death against the stone walls or throw herself into the well. The king knew that losing Kamvati wouldn't save Sattu. The spirit would only move on to haunt another house, possess another woman, and demand the same sacrifice.

"Bring Sattu to me," it would whisper, "and show me the **Lasso.**"

The scene was thick with tension, an air of unease threading through the corridors of the palace. Each shadow seemed deeper, each whispered sound sharper as the day approached a night that promised only dread. It had been weeks since Queen Kamvati had first started muttering, her soft voice turning harsh as she called, "**Lasso... lasso... lasso...**" while pounding her head against the cold stone walls. The desperation in her eyes mirrored a fear that no amount of royal power could quell. King Mandu, ruler of a kingdom haunted by legends and curses, watched helplessly as the woman he loved was torn apart from within.

The elders had once promised him freedom from this curse; priests had assured the king that no shadow of an old spirit would fall upon his house. Yet now, with Kamvati's eyes hollow and her voice an echo of madness, those reassurances dissolved into nothing. The whispers of "**Lasso Kumbh,**" the ritual rumored to bring life back from death, pierced through his mind. No one had ever completed it successfully—always, the end came with blood and broken bodies.

King Mandu knew what the ritual demanded: the sacrifice of an innocent child. The thought made his heart clench painfully, for the child this time would be none other than his son, Sattu. With a deep breath and trembling hands, he decreed preparations for the ritual. The entire palace assembled, the great hall crowded with fearful eyes and quivering lips. The heavy silence was broken only by Kamvati's unending chant, "Send him up... send Sattu up."

Sattu was brought forth, his small, bewildered face peering out from under a cloak. Mandu watched, eyes wet with a father's love and king's torment. He knew the moment the ritual began, Sattu would ascend the rope tied to a sacred urn. But once above, the unthinkable happened—Sattu's innocent face contorted as if grasping some unseen force, and he began to dismember himself. A muffled cry from the king's throat was drowned by the gasps of the crowd. Piece by piece, Sattu's small form fell to the floor, lifeless and cold.

Grief crushed Mandu like a wave. He swore an oath then, never to attempt such black magic again, and resolved never to father another child. His life became an echo of that night, each day hollow, as Kamvati's heart, too, crumbled. Unable to bear the weight of guilt, she flung herself into the well that had become infamous among the people, the dark pit where many desperate women had ended their lives.

Years passed like shadows over Mandu's once-vibrant eyes. Then came the news that shattered the fragile peace: someone had spoken the name **"Lasso Kumbh"** within the king's earshot. He bolted upright, demanding, "Who dares speak of it? Who seeks that cursed magic?"

A messenger trembled as he reported, "Two figures, Your Majesty. An old man and a child, cloaked and silent, wish to demonstrate the ritual to you."

Mandu's heart, scarred by loss, stirred with a flicker of hope. "Bring them at once!" he commanded, breath quickening. When the pair arrived, the king's eyes filled with tears. The child, veiled head to toe, made Mandu's voice shake. "Sattu... is it you, my son?"

But before he could move, the old man—a figure bearing the unmistakable presence of vaayun, who had vanished years ago—stepped forward. "Majesty, this child is not Sattu, but the key to saving many sons like him."

Mandu's hope crashed into bewilderment. The courtiers, eyes wide with shared pain, listened as vaayun continued, "If this ritual is performed correctly, no child will need to suffer again." The king's tears fell freely, disbelief battling with the whisper of hope in his chest. "You come here, after all this time, to show me salvation?" Vaayun nodded solemnly. "Allow us to proceed, but first, send all men out of the hall. Only women, especially those expecting children, must stay."

The king, surprised, demanded, "Why such conditions? Must I, too, leave?"

Vaayun glanced at the child, whose silence spoke volumes. "Yes, Majesty, only women can remain."

Despite the murmurs, Mandu consented. Guards ushered men out until the great hall was filled only with women, curiosity mingling with fear. The old man and the cloaked child prepared the golden circle at the center. The ritual began, a chant rising as Vaayun wove a sacred mantra through the air. The rope, tied to the urn, ascended as if guided by unseen hands.

The child climbed, step by silent step, and as he did, Mandu's heart cracked open. His gaze locked on the child's feet, strange and clawed like a beast's. Horror etched itself on the king's face. "Chamera!" he gasped, the name echoing through the chamber. Panic erupted as the women fled. Chamera, the cursed offspring of Queen Mayra, bore the form of a demon, his tale whispered through generations as a warning of wrathful gods.

Rushing forward, Mandu reached to stop the ritual, only to find vaayun standing in his way. "Calm yourself, Your Majesty. He is not a monster but a savior."

Before Vaayun could finish, the king's sword flashed. The elder crumpled, blood pooling beneath him. Above, Chamera's tears soaked the rope, weakening it as the world below erupted into chaos. The king, seizing his chance, cut the rope, sending Chamera spiraling out of sight.

And thus, the tale spread, of the monstrous boy who tried to bring peace to Mandu but disappeared into the heavens. The women of Mandu still light oil lamps on dark moonless nights, burying winged insects in the earth, an offering to soothe the soul of the child who sought redemption in the face of wrath.

Such is the legend of Mandu, the kingdom haunted by curses, shadowed by grief, and warmed by the silent memory of sacrifice.

CHAPTER SEVEN

Lasso, the Magician of Mandu

Gaurakhi bowed in gratitude to Dharmpal, touching his feet in reverence. As he rose, he spoke with deep emotion, his voice filled with respect and realization:

"Meeting you today feels like the culmination of my entire journey. You may not realize it, but you have shown me the path I was meant to walk, as though this village had been waiting for me all along. Your kindness and generosity have saved me from losing my way. I now understand much, but there are still questions that linger in my mind, questions I must find answers to before I can truly move forward."

The first question that troubled Gaurakhi's mind was why Chamera had invited so many women and kept the men away. Why had he placed the pregnant women so close to the magic rituals? If Chamera could perform such powerful magic, why reveal it in front of the king? Why not somewhere else? There were too many questions, too many mysteries. Without answers, he felt unable to proceed further.

Dharmpal, listening quietly, responded, "This is all I know. The same questions have troubled me as well. I never understood the role of women or why he performed his magic in the presence of the king. Why was it necessary?"

With these words, Gaurakhi bid farewell to Dharmpal and set off on his journey once more. The questions gnawed at him, and he felt an increasing sense of urgency. He had no clear answers yet, but something deep inside him told him that the answers lay ahead in the dense forest where Chamera had once spent so much time.

Gaurakhi knew in his heart that Chamera was a devout follower of Lord Shiva, a worshiper whose devotion had shaped both his body and mind in unimaginable ways. Gaurakhi's belief in Chamera grew stronger each day. Like Chamera, Gaurakhi too began to find solace in the solitude of the forest, where the whispers of nature seemed to speak directly to his soul. The days passed. Weeks turned into months. With each passing day, Gaurakhi became more deeply immersed in his devotion to Shiva. He found completeness in his worship, and within the jungle, he discovered a profound connection to the divine. Yet, as his devotion deepened, his thoughts kept drifting back to Chamera and the puzzle that remained unsolved.

Gaurakhi often reflected on a crucial remark Dharmpal had made: "Chamera did not think about just one thing at a time; he could think of many things, and he understood not just human nature but the forces of nature itself."

This thought gnawed at Gaurakhi's mind. "Chamera did not focus on one place, one moment; he understood many places, many things, all at once. He grasped the very essence of nature."

Gaurakhi felt the truth of this realization spreading through him. His hair stood on end, as if he were beginning to understand something profound—something about Chamera's mind, his life, and the path he had followed.

As he wandered deeper into the forest, near a river, surrounded by trees, animals, and plants, a thought began to take shape in Gaurakhi's mind. Could it be? Could this be the place where Chamera had worshiped Lord Shiva? It felt right. This was where Gaurakhi would find the answers he sought.

"Perhaps," he thought, "this is where Chamera worshiped Shiva. This is where the river, the earth, the creatures, and everything connected to nature came together. Shiva is here, in this place. The path to understanding him lies here."

Determined, Gaurakhi began to search the area. After days of wandering, tired and fatigued, he sat down to rest. As he lay down to sleep, his hand brushed against something hard. It felt like a stone. He reached down and discovered a small, weathered stone, shaped like a Shiva Lingam, covered in layers of sandalwood.

"This must be it," he thought. "This is the Lingam Chamera used to worship Shiva."

With renewed vigor, Gaurakhi began to dig around the stone. Two days later, he uncovered a large Shiva Lingam, not a small one, but one of considerable size. The Lingam was covered with thick layers of sandalwood paste. Gaurakhi knelt down and offered his prayers to the Lord, thanking him for guiding him to this moment. He knew now that he was very close to the answers he had been seeking.

As Gaurakhi continued to examine the area, he uncovered a hidden treasure beneath the stone: a collection of coins, clay statues, and old utensils. Most surprisingly, he found several ancient manuscripts, perhaps five or six in total, written in Sanskrit on wooden leaves. These manuscripts were covered in intricate script.

Gaurakhi carefully cleaned the manuscripts and began reading them. What he found astonished him. The stories of Chamera were deeper than he had ever imagined. These manuscripts were filled with knowledge that stretched far beyond what he had learned from Dharmpal or the village elders. The symbols and the letters seemed to weave together a story that defied conventional understanding.

It took Gaurakhi an entire month to decipher the ancient scripts. Each manuscript led to the next, and in order, they revealed the mystery that had eluded him for so long. The writings spoke of a time when kingdoms and realms were embroiled in constant battles, and one kingdom—Magadha—was on the rise.

Magadha, under the rule of King Suryamal, had defeated many kingdoms: Avanti, Ujjain, Taxila, and Gandhar. But their greatest challenge lay in conquering Anga Pradesh, ruled by the wise and revered King Suryamal. Despite repeated attempts, Magadha had always failed to defeat Anga, for Anga was a prosperous kingdom, and Suryamal was no ordinary king. He was a master strategist, respected even by his enemies.

But Magadha was relentless, and it began to look for a weakness in Anga. King Suryamal's greatest concern was the protection of his people, especially the women and children, for he could not bear the thought of them suffering. His mind, filled with compassion, led him to make a difficult decision.

He sent all the women and children of Anga Pradesh to Mandu Village, a secluded place deep in the forests, surrounded by jungle. The women and children, under the royal decree, made their way to Mandu in the dead of night, quietly and cautiously, to escape the looming threat of war.

Mandu, a village hidden within the dense jungles, became a refuge. The king instructed his men to guard it well, and for eight years, the women and children lived in safety, away from the turmoil of the outside world.

As time passed, a mysterious young man began visiting Mandu once a month, accompanied by a young child. He performed magical rituals that captivated the women and children. His name was Lasso. No one knew his true identity, but the villagers came to know him as Lasso, the magician. Each time he arrived, the village would buzz with excitement. The women would eagerly gather to witness his mystical performances, which were always held during the new moon.

Lasso would tie a rope to a pot, and, with a wave of his hand, would lift it into the air. Then, he would make his child perform strange feats, making him float and dance in the air. The women and children would dance with joy, their spirits lifted by the magic. Over time, the legend of Lasso spread far and wide, and his fame grew throughout the surrounding villages.

But the peace in Mandu could not last forever. As the Magadha empire grew stronger, its sights turned toward Anga Pradesh once more. Magadha had already crushed many kingdoms, and now it sought to defeat Anga. The king of Anga, knowing that war was inevitable, took solace in the fact that the women and children in Mandu were safe. The soldiers of Anga were dying, but the future of the kingdom—their children—remained secure.

Then, one fateful day, news reached the king. Magadha's army had attacked Mandu. The soldiers cut off the heads of all the women, and mercilessly slaughtered the children as well. Some women tried to escape by hiding in wells, but the soldiers found them, and even the wells were not safe.

The bloodshed was unimaginable.

The king, upon hearing the tragic news, collapsed in despair. He could not speak, his body trembling with grief. He had lost everything—the women, the children, the future of Anga Pradesh. The sanctity of Mandu had been shattered, and all hope was lost.

In this final moment of despair, the king realized the terrible cost of war, and how the lives of innocents were always the first to be sacrificed. Anga Pradesh had fallen, and with it, any hope for the future.

CHAPTER EIGHT

The Secrets of Betrayal

As King Suryamal entered Mandu, his heart sank at the sight of the carnage around him. He saw the lifeless bodies of women and children scattered across the village, their souls extinguished by the ruthless attack. The massacre had broken his spirit, and he was shattered from within. He felt helpless, devastated by the horror he witnessed. His mind, once sharp and resolute, now faltered in the face of this unimaginable tragedy.

King Suryamal turned to his trusted general, Kanthak, for answers. "How could this have happened with you here? How did we fail to protect them?" he asked, his voice strained with disbelief.

Kanthak, ever pragmatic, responded, "There were many of them, Maharaj, and only a few of us. Moreover, they struck during the night when we were least prepared."

But King Suryamal, though weary, could sense something more sinister at play. He suspected that someone had informed Magadha of their secret refuge in Mandu. "Find out who leaked this information to Magadha," the king ordered, his voice cold with determination.

Kanthak's investigation soon led to a disturbing discovery. A young man, who went by the name of *Lasso*, had been visiting Mandu every new moon for the past two years. He would come with a young child, and though no one knew his true identity, he was famous in the village for performing strange magic—referred to as the *Lasso Kumbh*. This young man had earned a reputation for enchanting the women and children with his supernatural displays, making them believe he could defy the laws of nature.

King Suryamal, still unsure about Lasso's true intentions, decided to wait for the next new moon to investigate further. When Lasso arrived again, as expected, with his child in tow, the king decided to confront him.

"Many people have spoken highly of your talents," Suryamal said, addressing Lasso. "Tell me, what magic do you perform for these people? I've heard that today, the women wish to see you perform your *Lasso Kumbh* magic for me. Let us see what you can do."

Lasso, pleased by the king's attention, prepared for his performance. He took out his rope and began the ritual. "This is my magic, Maharaj," he said confidently. "Watch as the rope rises." The rope stood up straight, seemingly defying gravity.

The king, intrigued but skeptical, asked, "Is this rope truly strong enough to hold more than one person? Could it carry a man as well as a child?"

Lasso, smiling, responded, "Why, yes, Maharaj. If you wish, you could send ten soldiers up the rope. It would hold them all."

King Suryamal, though hesitant, decided to test the limits of Lasso's magic. "Let us see if your magic is truly as powerful as you claim. I will send one soldier, but he will be equal to one hundred men," the king declared. He gestured to Kanthak, signaling him to climb the rope.

Kanthak, following the king's orders, climbed the rope and immediately noticed how strong and unyielding it was. He marveled at its strength. But then, with a swift gesture from the king, Kanthak cut the rope right where Lasso's son was perched, high up in the air. Lasso's son, who had been joyfully performing tricks on the rope, began to fall. His small body tumbled down, breaking apart as it hit the ground.

Lasso was horrified at the sight. He screamed in anguish as his child's body fell to the earth. "No! Not my son!" he cried out, his voice filled with despair. He turned to the king, begging for an explanation.

Suryamal, his expression cold, said, "This is your fate. Tell me who you are, and what you did to bring this destruction to Mandu. You have betrayed us, and now all the women and children are dead, slaughtered by Magadha's soldiers because of you."

Lasso, unable to bear the grief of losing his child and knowing the devastation he had caused, could not respond. His voice was choked with tears. But before he could speak, Kanthak approached from behind and, in one swift motion, severed Lasso's tongue.

"Enough," Kanthak said, his voice harsh and unforgiving. "This traitor's tongue will no longer spread lies. He won't speak again, nor will he ever be able to cast his magic again." With that, Kanthak dragged Lasso into the jungle, leaving him to suffer for his betrayal.

Lasso, now broken and mute, was left to wander the wilds, consumed by grief. He could not bear the thought of his son's death, nor the pain of knowing that his actions had led to the massacre of innocent women and children.

His mind was torn between guilt and sorrow, unable to reconcile the destruction he had caused.

In the meantime, Neelu, a young woman from Mandu who had witnessed Kanthak's cruelty, knew the truth. Neelu had seen how Kanthak mistreated the women of Mandu, exploiting them and using his power to silence anyone who dared to speak out. She knew that Kanthak had been a key player in the tragedy, enabling Magadha's soldiers to carry out the attack without resistance.

Neelu had also been a victim of Kanthak's abuse. He had harassed her, and when she had tried to speak out, he had threatened her life. One day, after Kanthak had subjected her to one of his violent attacks, Neelu decided that she could no longer stay silent. She wrote down everything she had witnessed—the truth about Kanthak's actions, about the betrayal of Lasso, and about the massacre of the women and children.

Neelu had planned to take this information to the king, to expose Kanthak's role in the tragedy, but Kanthak was always watching. When he discovered her intentions, he sent his soldiers after her, determined to stop her from revealing the truth. Desperate, Neelu fled and hid in a well, hoping that the soldiers would not find her.

Though Neelu was able to escape for a time, her fate remained uncertain. She could not carry the truth to King Suryamal, and the horrors of Mandu seemed destined to remain shrouded in secrecy. Kanthak's tyranny continued unchecked, and the suffering of the innocent women and children of Mandu became a silent, forgotten tragedy.

CHAPTER NINE

The Final Revelation

As soon as Kanthak felt that the situation was becoming precarious, he sent word to Magadha. The response from Magadha was swift and ruthless—they turned Mandu into a graveyard. The once vibrant and thriving village was now a desolate, silent wasteland, its inhabitants slaughtered without mercy.

Neelu, aware of the horrific truth, decided to go to the king and inform him of Kanthak's treachery. However, she knew the danger of speaking out. If she couldn't reach the king, she had a plan to ensure the truth was preserved. Neelu buried everything she knew in a clay pot, etching the details into it, and hid it carefully, hoping that someone would discover it if she failed.

As expected, Kanthak learned of Neelu's plan to reveal the truth to the king. Desperate to silence her, he pursued Neelu relentlessly. In her attempt to escape, Neelu fell into a well and drowned, her life extinguished by the very forces she had sought to expose.

But Neelu's story did not end there. She had left behind the clay pot, and in it was a message—written by her hand and later discovered by a wise scholar named Gaurakhi. The pot contained the last piece of the puzzle, the final piece of Neelu's tragic journey.

The final message, inscribed in the clay pot, read:

"I know everything now. Kanthak, in his cruelty, tortured Lasso and then buried him alive beneath the king's palace. But the truth of Kanthak's actions has remained hidden. Perhaps this spirit—the ghost of Lasso—will reveal Kanthak's true nature to the world. Lasso's soul seeks justice, and that is why, every new moon, the *Lasso Kumbh* performance takes place in the village. It is the spirit's way of drawing attention to the truth."

Upon reading this, Gaurakhi took a deep breath, realizing the gravity of what had happened. He now understood the mystery behind the repeated *Lasso Kumbh* performances and why they always occurred on the night of the new moon. It was not mere magic—it was the curse of Lasso's spirit, seeking justice and trying to expose Kanthak's dark deeds.

Gaurakhi had learned the truth. He now knew that Kanthak's cruelty could not go unpunished. The spirit of Lasso was not something that could be destroyed or banished. As Chamera had written in the final message, the ghost of Lasso had become vengeful after his death. It had been summoned by Kanthak's betrayal, and it sought to expose the truth of his actions to the world.

For years, Kanthak had evaded justice, but Lasso's spirit had grown increasingly restless and vengeful. In fact, whenever the king had performed his magic in the past, Lasso's ghost had appeared, causing chaos and fear, seeking to remind everyone of the king's and Kanthak's sins.

Gaurakhi understood now. He knew what path to follow. Should he follow the route his father had taught him, or should he take the one laid out by the spirit of Chamera? He sat in deep contemplation for several days, wrestling with his thoughts. After a few days, he decided to go to the jungle and meditate on Lord Shiva, seeking clarity and strength for the journey ahead.

Days turned into weeks, and Gaurakhi spent more time reflecting on his father's teachings. He finally decided to take the path that had been shown to him by Chamera, who had understood the need to confront Kanthak's evil directly.

Gaurakhi had come to the painful realization that Lasso's spirit could never be laid to rest. As Chamera had written, this was a spirit that sought the truth above all else. And now, after Chamera's death, the spirit had grown even more restless and vengeful. There had been multiple instances when the king had tried to silence the ghost by killing those who performed magic, even beheading them during rituals. But every time, the spirit of Lasso became more furious.

The ghost had become corrupted and vengeful over time, and Gaurakhi knew that the task before him was not simple. It would be very difficult to deal with the powerful spirit, now twisted with rage.

Gaurakhi, however, was determined. He resolved to confront the curse of Lasso's spirit and find a way to break the cycle. He felt a deep sense of urgency, knowing that time was running out. He needed to find a way to confront Kanthak's dark past, and in doing so, perhaps, release the restless spirit of Lasso from its vengeance. Gaurakhi knew that he had to find a way to break the chain of events set in motion by Kanthak's treachery, to cut through the cycles of time that had been woven together by the curse.

In his heart, Gaurakhi could feel the weight of the past, the burden of Neelu's untold story, and the restless soul of Lasso that still haunted the land. He had made up his mind: he would face the curse head-on, whatever the cost.

Inner sound of Gaurakhi –

(You have recognized yourself. Now the penance of me, Gayatri, and **Vetalbhadra** has come to fruition. The end of this dark power will occur within the timeframe of one and a half years. During this time, you must immerse yourself in the ashes to endure this power.

To counter this magic, the man must recite the mantra of Vetalbhadra. You will need to place the ashes into a pot to contain the dark power. When the man goes to prepare the pot, he should keep the ashes there. As the pot is being prepared, the warmth from the ashes will spread. When this pot is cooked, the ashes inside will generate heat, and this heat will create a burning sensation within you. You must endure this power, and the mark on your body will be significant. It will be a time when your soul will separate from your body. At that moment, when you are facing the opposite direction of time, you will have transformed into ashes. Someone will need to keep the ashes safe.....)

Gaurakhi was trapped in a dilemma. What should he do to turn back the Wheel of Time engraved upon his back? Thoughts swirled endlessly in his mind—the words of the little girl who had come seeking his help echoed within him. She had told him that the Wheel of Time burned upon his back, and that he must use it to step into the past, to merge with the Gaurakhi of a time long gone. But how? The question gnawed at his very being.

Sitting in silence, Gaurakhi delved deep into his thoughts. Memories that did not belong to just one Gaurakhi but to many pulsed within him. He now understood—he was Gayatri's son, but his existence had been prolonged unnaturally by the very Wheel upon his back. He had died countless times, only to be resurrected again and again. Each time death claimed him, another

Gaurakhi from the future had stepped into his body, keeping him alive.

He knew this much—there was a purpose, a grand reason behind it all. The end of Chamera. But how? And why had all the Gaurakhis chosen him? That much, at least, was clear—he was the result of Vetalbhadra's illusion and the divine penance of Gaurakhnath. He had been born to end this dark magic. But the means to do so remained unknown.

Gaurakhi closed his eyes, sinking into deep meditation. The answer lay in time itself. This magic could only be undone in Chamera's era. He had to awaken the Gaurakhi of that time, step into his body, and arrive at the moment when the sorcery was first cast.

But how? How was he to reverse the Wheel of Time? That singular question burned within him, consuming him from the inside.

Gaurakhi was lost in thought, searching for a way to turn the Wheel of Time in the opposite direction. His mind wrestled with the puzzle, seeking an answer that remained elusive. As he sat in contemplation, his gaze fell upon a group of children playing with the earth, molding shapes from the soil with innocent delight. A wave of nostalgia washed over him, carrying him back to his own childhood—the days when he, too, had played in the dust, letting its scent and texture fill him with joy. He had loved the earth so dearly that his mother had tied a small amulet filled with sacred soil around his neck, believing it to hold a special power.

That memory came rushing back, vivid and untouched by time. He remembered the day he had once attempted to untie the amulet, curious to see the soil it contained. But before he could, his mother's voice had rung out sharply, stopping him in his tracks. "Do not open it, my son! This is no ordinary soil—it carries the blessing of Vetalbhadra himself!" she had warned. Whenever Gaurakhi had questioned her about the amulet, she had always answered him with the same tale—a story of a man who had once held a handful of earth and, through its power, had traveled across time to meet his mother who had died twenty years before. A story of a love so boundless that even death could not sever it.

Hearing this story as a child, Gaurakhi had often embraced his mother, feeling the weight of its meaning in his heart. And now, at last, he understood—his mother was none other than Gayatri. This realization brought a soft smile to his lips, a quiet acknowledgment of the truth he had long sought.

But as he lingered in these thoughts, another revelation struck him, one hidden within his mother's tale. She had always insisted that the amulet contained Vetalbhadra's blessing and that the man in the story had turned the Wheel of Time to see his mother again. The connection was clear now.

Gaurakhi reached for the amulet at his throat. His fingers trembled as he untied it, holding it in his palm with reverence. The answer had been with him all along. Now, he knew exactly what he had to do.

A son adopts the ways of his father, but here Gaurakhi chooses to diverge from Madhav's path, using the ashes of his meditation to traverse time, landing in the era where Chamera's magic is at its peak. This decision by Gaurakhi astounded everyone, but could a true devotee of Shiva ever be wrong? Gaurakhi descends precisely when Chamera is performing his magic, leaving the gathered crowd stunned.

Story always left a path open—a mysterious route shrouded in the fog of possibility. Gaurakhi, armed with his ascetic wisdom, often turned to his profound powers in moments of need. From his neck, he untied a small pouch, withdrew it, and began chanting a sacred mantra. Slowly, his physical form dissolved into ashes. This act wasn't one of destruction but transformation—a shift into a state that defied the ordinary rules of existence. Now, he was ready to journey into the past, where time itself felt pliable, and impossible became possible.

As Gaurakhi prepared for this temporal voyage, his father's teachings echoed in his mind. Yet, within his heart, a different determination stirred—one deeply personal, untainted by the expectations of legacy. This mission was his alone, driven by a purpose uniquely his.

There was a limitation to Gaurakhi's power: he could only inhabit the body of his past self. This singular trait was both his greatest strength and his ultimate vulnerability. Resolute, he directed his consciousness to the moment in history where the unfolding events awaited his intervention.

In the past, the Gaurakhi of that time—unknowingly sharing space with his future self—felt a strange awakening. Fleeting shadows danced at the edges of his awareness, like the whispers of a half-remembered dream. Slowly, he rose, as though a radiant light had pierced the veil of his slumbering mind. Compelled by an unseen force, he began walking toward Mandu village, toward the royal court where a gathering of women had been summoned.

But the Gaurakhi of the present, now inhabiting his former self, knew that something far darker was unfolding. He moved with urgency, his heart pounding with the weight of impending doom. Disguised, he arrived at the court, only to witness a chilling sight—the soul of Lasso attempting to merge with Chamera. The latter was performing a wild, mesmerizing dance, his movements a ritual offering. For Lasso, this union was a long-anticipated dream. Chamera, on the other hand, was a being of immense mental strength, burdened by a body that had always betrayed him. He yearned for physical power, and Lasso's essence seemed the answer.

Yet Chamera's longing was layered with pain and anger. Once a devoted follower of Shiva, he had sought the god's blessings in vain. His connections to Vayu and Vishva, once sources of wisdom and strength, had been severed. Even his mother had been cruelly taken from him. Chamera's mind, sharp and calculating, saw this moment as a rare opportunity—a chance to rewrite his destiny.

As Lasso's soul began merging with Chamera's body, Gaurakhi arrived. But he was too late. The king, foreseeing the danger, had already cut the sacred rope tethering the ritual to its completion. Yet half of Lasso's soul had already found refuge in Chamera, creating a hybrid form of unimaginable power. Chamera and Gaurakhi clashed, their confrontation a battle not just of strength but of will and ancient knowledge.

Desperate, Gaurakhi chanted a mantra intended to weaken Chamera's form, for only a weakened body could be defeated. But the attempt faltered. Lasso's partial presence had fortified Chamera beyond Gaurakhi's expectations. The past's Gaurakhi, unable to fully comprehend the advanced mantras his future self possessed, struggled to hold his form. The strain of channeling such energy shattered his body. Blood trickled from his ears as he collapsed to the ground, lifeless.

All that remained was ash, faintly glowing embers surrounded by rising smoke. From these ashes, the soil began to gather—as if the earth itself mourned, pulling the remnants of Gaurakhi into its embrace. And thus, Gaurakhi's form dissolved into the very elements he sought to transcend, leaving behind only silence and a sense of unfinished fate.

Epilogue

Gaurakhi lay on the ground, his breath shallow and uneven. The world around him, once so vast and full of purpose, now seemed distant. The weight of centuries bore down on him, as though time itself had wrapped him in its unyielding grip. His body, a vessel of weariness, could not withstand the agony of the chakra embedded in his back. His voice, raspy and faint, echoed through the silent air.

"I feel so weak now... this wheel... it must be the wheel of time. A cycle I never truly understood. The pain... from the chakra on my back, I can no longer bear it. I realize now... this wheel was bringing future Gaurakhis into my time, allowing me to survive all these years... The burning sensation, it spins like a clock—always turning in a clockwise motion. This pain... it was meant to merge with the Gaurakhis of the future. That's why, when I first felt the presence of Gaurakhnath Dev, he told me, 'Without understanding the soul's journey, you must not take a step...'

His body trembled, unable to withstand the agony. "Ahh... ahhh... this pain... it's unbearable... I turned the wheel in an anticlockwise direction... I can't take it anymore... Help me... Please... The pain... it's too much... the wheel... it's now spinning in the opposite direction..."

The words faded into the wind, and with a final, agonized cry, Gaurakhi collapsed. The chakra, once so tightly wound around him, seemed to unravel. The wheel of time, having held him for so long, finally ceased its turn. The last traces of Gaurakhi's existence—his body, his essence, his struggle—dispersed into the air, turning to ash.

And so, he was gone. His journey, which had spanned across time and space, had come to its end. The world he once knew was left to continue, unaware of the sacrifice he had made, the pain he had endured. Yet, somewhere beyond the fabric of time, the echoes of his existence would remain—forever intertwined with the timeless cycle that had defined his life.

As the winds carried away his ashes, the chakra lay still, its power dormant for the moment, but its journey was far from over.

As the dust of Gaurakhi's existence settled, the silence that followed was almost sacred. The winds whispered, carrying with them the weight of a thousand years. And in that stillness, time itself seemed to speak—its voice soft but undeniable.

"Someone once spoke the truth about me, " it said. "That time's march is its shield. "The words hung in the air, a reflection of the eternal truth that had guided Gaurakhi's life—through the pain, the trials, and the cycles that had never ceased. Time, like a vast and unyielding force, had been both his weapon and his protector, shaping his fate, and ultimately, bringing him to his final moment.

And now, as the cycle of his life ended, time stood still for just a moment. The shield, once wielded by Gaurakhi to defy the inevitable, now lay dormant, knowing that its work had been done.

As the world continued its endless turning, oblivious to the passing of one soul, the truth of time's power lingered in the shadows. The cycle would continue, but for now, there was only quiet. And in that quiet, time's voice echoed softly—reassured, eternal, and ever-present